Danny's

Choice

FOR LITERARY HEAT

www.barbarianspy.com

WARNING: This book is for sale to **ADULT AUDIENCES ONLY**. Contains graphic gay male sex, reluctance, multiple partners, anal sex, nongraphic violence, and gay love all of which may be considered offensive by some readers.

All sexually active characters in this work are at least 18 years of age.

BarbarianSpy
Toronto
Australia

Danny's Choice

by

HABU

Table of Contents

Introduction

The story of the casting couch as an avenue to stardom, whether on New York's Broadway or in Hollywood, is a classic one in literature and film. *Danny's Choice* plays and twists this theme. It is about predatory producers and the hard bargains they strike to further the careers of young men in exchange for the men's virginity. It is about how this effects the lives of those young men.

Danny's Choice is a collection of four interlocking stories—sometimes connected directly and sometimes only in coincidence. As part of the twist, *Danny's Choice*, within the context of the stories, is also a fictitious book written by the fictitious Christopher Wilson in the late 1950s about his coming of age into the gay lifestyle in New York City in the post-World War II decade between 1947 and 1957.

In some contexts within these stories *Danny's Choice* is being constructed before the reader's eyes. In some stories it has been optioned to be filmed in the mid 1960s as an underground, but major production, graphic gay art film. And various protagonists in the stories are either the author of the book, the inspiration for the book, or young men willing to give up their bodies to play the lead in the film taken from the book.

In some cases the reader will encounter the same circumstance told from different perspectives, or a scenario so familiar that it *must* be a direct connection to another scenario—but isn't necessarily such. It's up to the reader to decide who is doing what.

Second Chances

Chris Wilson became aware of a change in the pattern of the gurgling sound of the respirator across the bedroom in the king-sized bed. Knowing this signaled that Earl would be awake—and perhaps even that he was trying to get attention—Chris put his pen down and turned to look in that direction. He had been at the desk at the window overlooking the turning circle of Broadway producer Earl Youngblood's Long Island mansion. He was reviewing what he'd written of the fiction piece he was writing—novel, novella, short story, or confessional, he didn't know yet—for the umpteenth time. It was, he thought, the key passage in the work. He wanted to get it right.

Earl indeed did appear to be awake. He was on his back and the respirator mask was on his face, but his face was turned toward the window. Chris had no idea how long the elderly man had been watching him. A cursory inspection, though, told Chris why.

The sheet over Earl's midsection was tented. Chris' attentions were needed. He stood and looked out the bedroom window. There was no sign yet of Kenton Walsh's impending arrival. The only activity that Chris could see at the front of the estate were the two gardeners, father and son, Thadeus and Jeremiah, working to smooth out the lines of the boxwood hedges in the center of the turning circle. He would like to stay at the window and watch the two black men work—they were both muscular and handsome men, although the father was a bit grizzled—but Earl's needs always came first.

He moved over to the bed, pulling up the straight chair that backed up to the wall next to it, and placed it beside the bed. Before sitting down in the chair, Chris, pulled the mask off Earl's face just long enough to lean over and kiss him on the lips. The hunger of Earl's kiss, even though he had to hold his breath to engage in it, was all Chris needed to know about what Earl needed—wanted. He replaced the mask, and, while still standing, he let a hand glide under the sheet at Earl's waist, take the elderly man's cock in hand, and begin stroking it. No matter what else ailed Earl, he still managed to produce and sustain a hard on.

Chris sat down in the chair then, leaned over Earl's body, brushed his pajama tops open, and began tonguing into the wispy gray matting on his chest, search for, and finding, in turn, one nipple and then the other. Earl had always liked the nipple play.

After a few minutes of this, Chris kissed down Earl's sternum and belly, pushed the sheet off his pelvis, opened his mouth over Earl's cock, and began the tonguing, sucking, and nipping play that Chris knew Earl wanted from him. It wasn't long before Earl's body jerked and he released his seed in a weak flow down Chris' throat.

The respirator gurgled away and guttural sounds came from under the mask that Chris associated with Earl expressing thanks. Chris wiped his lips off on the sheet, pulled it over Earl's now-flaccid cock, and returned to the desk at the window.

It had been thus with Earl Youngblood, the famous and powerful Broadway play producer for nearly three months now. This certainly wasn't the Earl Youngblood of old. A series of strokes had taken away much of his movement and all of his speech. But he was a strong old bird. Chris firmly believed that the old man's sex drive would be the last bodily function to desert him. Chris, at twenty-six, initially a dancer in off-Broadway productions, then a small-part actor in Broadway plays, and now nearly a full-time caretaker of his first lover, had been with Earl for over seven years, with the exception of a year and a half in the middle of the period during which Chris had gone astray.

Earl had taken him back, though.

Before sitting at the desk to look over the phrase in his story one more time, Chris went to the window and looked down into the turning circle at the entrance. Still no Jaguar. Ken told him he was driving a Jaguar now. Knowing that Earl had quietly and happily fallen asleep again and would not need Chris for at least a few hours, Chris lingered at the window, watching the gardeners work and keeping an eye out for the Jaguar sports car Ken had gushed about over the phone. He had proudly said he had picked off the last new 1957 Jaguar D-Type roadster to be produced and sent to the States to be put on display in a Manhattan car dealer's showroom. Ken, although living in Manhattan himself and having little use for a car in the city other than having bragging rights for it, had always gone for the flashy toys and possessions. As soon as that thought entered Chris' mind, he felt the sting of the reality of it. For a brief time, he'd been just such a possession.

After a few moments, he sat back at the desk and, with a sigh, picked up the now-tattered yellow legal pad he'd poured his heart out on, and a pen, and started yet another review of his story.

"Just settle down and stop pushing at me, Danny. I'm in now."

He wasn't in as far as he was going to get, I was soon to learn. The pain was excruciating, not least because it was so strange compared to anything I'd experienced before. But I'd been assured that it would lessen and that, eventually, I usually wouldn't notice it much at all—not compared with the pleasure it would be giving me. And there was some of that already. The expectation of it; the "it's finally happening" of it.

"Stop pushing on me. I'm in. You're fucked already. Got your cherry. No reason to fight it. Open to me and enjoy it. You're a dancer. Dance on the cock."

I was on all fours on the studio couch in his office—the proverbial casting couch—and he was standing behind me, between my calves that jutted out over the end of the couch. I had twisted around and swung an arm behind me, the palm of my hand extending through his open and separated dress shirt and pushing at his muscular, hairy chest. I was bearing the weight of my twisted torso on a fist buried in the surface of the couch. He was crouched behind me, his hands gripping my hips, his dick inside me. Only a few inches, it turned out. He was going to be much deeper than that soon.

I know I was giving him a wild look. The look in his eyes was one of determination and of being a bit perturbed. I know I was crying out something, but I was trying my best that it not be a demand for him to stop. He wasn't raping me. I'd agreed to it— I'd agreed to it months earlier, in fact. It's just that now it was happening, it was overwhelming.

"Oh, for Christ sake," he growled. And I felt the hands leave my hips and he was twisting

around to the nearby chair that he'd hung his coat over. The hands came back with a long, cashmere neck scarf, which he whipped over my head; pulling my wrists together, causing me to collapse my chest on the surface of the couch—my tail still in the air, still skewered by his dick—and tying my wrists together with it. . . .

A car horn from beyond the window interrupted Chris' review. He hadn't changed a word, though. He hadn't changed a word in the last several readings. He read it now more to connect with memories. Of course Chris never could get anything like this published. Certainly not in this era of the buttoned-down late '50s when, as Chris well knew, there was a suppressed sexuality bubbling under the surface but a thick puritanical veneer on top. And, as he also well knew, it was whoever was on top who controlled. And, perhaps more true, it would never get published because it exposed the ways of predatory theater producers.

Outside was a Jaguar roadster convertible, just as Chris was expecting. Thadeus and Jeremiah had stopped clipping the hedge and were standing there in awe of the vehicle. It was exactly what Chris had expected Ken to be driving. And the flamboyant actor popped out of it, over the door without opening it, just as Chris would have expected from him. Chris was sure Ken saw the maneuver in some British movie and had used it himself ever since. Always the "look at me" actor. He probably was completely unaware that, as tall and broad-shouldered as he was, he looked altogether too large for the car.

But he looked good. Chris hadn't seen him in over four years. Earl hadn't taken Chris back to Broadway in that time. Ken was taboo around here when Earl was himself, although Earl and Ken had worked with each other, by mutual need, when Earl was in New York. Ken had always looked like the leading man, tall, well built, elegantly thin, expensively dressed, and with those killer blue eyes, flashy white teeth, beach tan, and curly auburn hair. Mr. Self-Confidence himself.

He must have sensed that Chris was watching him from a second-floor window, because he swept the beret he was wearing from his head and did a curtain-call bow to the very window Chris was standing at.

Chris opened the double window, leaned out, and called down, "I'll be down in just a minute."

He had a bit of an idea why Ken had come at this moment, but Chris would be damned if they would greet each other over the prone and gurgling body of Earl Youngblood. Chris could have just refused the visit, but he assumed Ken wouldn't leave it there—that Chris would have to face this sooner or later.

Beyond the door into the corridor, Chris nodded to the no-nonsense nurse who, clicking away with knitting needles, was sitting in a club chair that had been set against the wall by the door. She nodded back, stuck the needles in a ball of thread, rose, and brushed by him into the room. This had become a regular arrangement. Round-the-clock nursing service had been laid on, but when Chris was in the bedroom with Earl, the nurse took up station in the corridor, leaving the two men alone. This included the nighttime hours, because Chris still slept in the king-size bed with Earl—usually giving Earl the comfort that he still craved and holding the man in his arms and whispering to him of good times past as Earl drifted off to merciful sleep. A nurse was nearby, though, in anticipation of the day and hour she would be needed.

* * * *

"What is that?" Chris asked, indicating the two small suitcases—probably all that fit in the back of the Jaguar— Jeremiah was setting down behind Kenton Walsh in the foyer just inside the front door. Walsh was standing in front them, posing for Chris as the latter came down from the stairs.

"I heard about Earl. I have come to help you cope with his last days."

"Don't be dramatic, Ken," Chris said. "These aren't Earl's last days. He'll be fine. Don't think you'll be settling in." No way was Chris going to let Ken know how bad Earl's condition was.

"I must see him. Take me to him."

"I don't think so, Ken. I think that seeing you appear in his bedroom would be enough to kill him. I didn't tell him you were dropping in for a visit. I wouldn't have agreed to the visit if I'd known it involved suitcases."

"His bedroom?" Ken asked, a hopeful look on his face.

"Our bedroom," Chris shot back, "Earl's and mine." He saw that Jeremiah was standing there between the suitcases, magnificently black, but obviously out of his element inside the house. "Just leave them there, Jeremiah, thank you. You can go back to trimming the boxwood now."

So like Ken to commandeer service to avoid lifting a finger himself, Chris thought.

Ken was smiling, though, as Jeremiah backed out of the front door, leaving the suitcases where they were. A small win for him not having them returned directly to the car, certainly, but on the path to a victory nonetheless.

Chris looked away from him, realizing that he'd made a choice by not sending the suitcases right back. Ken was still irresistible in his own way after all these years. Completely exasperating, but irresistible anyway. Chris could feel the attraction of the man in his body—he had always found Ken arousing—and he walked down the stairs and around the banister and pointed himself toward the kitchen down the hall running beside the staircase so that

Ken couldn't see the effect he'd had. This undoubtedly was why Earl had kept Walsh at arms' length from Chris for the last four years.

"Come on through to the kitchen. I'll put the coffee on."

They didn't make it to the kitchen. In the shadow of the back hall, Ken caught up with Chris, backed him into the corridor wall, and pulled in close to him, pushing his knees into the wall on either side of Chris' thighs. He came in for a kiss before Chris could recover from the surprise of the boldness of the man.

Also because of the suddenness of the maneuver, Chris' lips yielded to the familiarity and melting nature of Ken's kiss. Ken grabbed Chris' wrists and raised and pushed the younger man's arms against the wall over his head. It was a hungry kiss from both men. But Chris recovered from the surprise, and Ken jerked his head back.

"Fuck. You bit my lip."

"You assumed too much, Ken. It's long over."

"I don't think so. I can feel you. You're hard. You want me. You're a slut for it."

"Maybe I want it, but we're beyond that now. I let you in before and you led me on and used me. I've made my choice."

"The old man's dying, Chris. Everyone says that. I've come to give you a second chance."

"You already were my second chance. You said you'd take me to Hollywood. That you had a leading role contracted out there, and you'd get me in the film too. I wouldn't have left Earl otherwise. You pulled me away from Earl, used me for over a year, and then, when you were called to Hollywood, I didn't go with you. There were no parts for me in Hollywood."

"You went back to Earl too soon. Earl got the better part of that deal. Got to fuck you and never let you rise above five lines of dialogue in a play. And from what I hear, he's been comatose for what, two or three months?"

"Three months. But not comatose."

"You can't go three months without a hard cock inside you, Chris. Don't fool me. You are aching for it. I feel you hard and trembling for it. You're going to let me fuck you, aren't you?—and take care of you while Earl's dying and then take you away from here, back to Hollywood, to resume what we had before."

"There are people in the house. We can't do this, Ken."

Ken came in for another kiss, and this time Chris gave into it completely.

"People? What people?" Ken asked. His hands came away from holding Chris' wrists above his head against the wall, and came down between them, unbuckling Chris' belt, unzipping him, pushing down on the waistband of the trousers and briefs so that they puddled down to the floor.

"God you're hard for it," he muttered, as he briefly got the measure of Chris' cock before palming the younger man's buttocks and spreading them, moving his two middle fingers to the rim of Chris' hole. "And opening right up for it. What people?"

The fingers penetrated the rim and Chris shuddered, but he didn't try to break free.

"Earl's nurse, the gardeners, Earl." His response was breathy. He already was panting.

"Appears to me that the gardeners never come in the house. And Earl? Seriously. We can be quiet if you aren't too vocal. Remember how you used to scream for it? We can chance the nurse, can't we?"

"Yes," Chris answered in a small voice. He brought his hands down and wrapped them around Ken's neck. He sheltered his cheek in the hollow of Ken's shoulder. He moaned as Ken rocked against his now-naked pelvis, showing Chris that Ken was very hard now too.

"I'm going to fuck you now," Ken growled. "Hook your legs on my hips. Roll your ass up to me."

"Yes," Chris answered, complying.

"You'll have to take it out and put it in yourself."

Chris complied, unzipping Ken's fly and fishing his hard cock out, trembling when he felt Ken was wearing no underwear.

Ken laughed, knowing why Chris had shuddered. "I knew you'd take me like this," he said. "You always did."

"Yes, I always did," Chris whispered. But to himself he was thinking, But I left you. I left you without a second thought when Earl was willing to take me back. And I'll be damned if I leave him again for you.

Despite his words, he placed the bulb of the cock in position and impaled himself on it. The battle then was one of working to stifle his cries of pleasure and taking as Ken moved deeper inside him, and thrust up, again and again, rubbing Chris' back up and down on the corridor wall with the power of the thrusting. Chris took the penetration in silence. He'd be damned if he'd give Ken the pleasure of knowing just how much he melted to having Ken's cock inside him again.

They held, but only briefly, after Ken ejaculated inside Chris, both of them panting hard, slowly cooling down. It hadn't been lost on Ken that Chris hadn't come. It had been agony for Chris not to do so, but he'd be damned too if he'd let Ken have that satisfaction. Chris was weak, but he could use that weakness to send a signal to Ken that Ken couldn't ignore.

Chris pushed Ken away, jerked up his briefs and trousers, and without giving Ken a second glance, turned and headed for the kitchen again. "Do you still take both cream and sugar in your coffee?" He'd kept the modulation of his voice as steady and matter-of-fact as he was trained as an actor to accomplish.

＊ ＊ ＊ ＊

They didn't meet again until dinner, where they sat miles apart from each other at the long table as a mature and jolly woman moved in and out of the kitchen and between them, serving the meal and chattering incessantly in a cheerful voice. If she discerned there was a chill in the air, she pretended not to know. The tension was like a long, drawn-out violin bowing—a bow ready to snap at any instant. A storm was raging outside, holding nothing back. That made the atmosphere in the dining room all that more apparent to the two diners.

When she was back in the kitchen, the first thing Ken, who had appeared confused and despondent during the service, said was, "You have a cook?"

"Yes, and there's a maid too. But neither of them was in the house when you arrived."

"Ah." Than after a long pause, "Chris—"

"It was thoughtful of you to check in on Earl and me, Ken. But, as you can see, we are doing fine and have all of our needs taken care of."

"All of your needs?" He gave Chris a sharp look. "I came here to give you a second chance."

"I've already answered that. You already were a second chance for me. You didn't come through on your promises. I'm with Earl now—wholly."

"You can't go without someone to fuck you, Chris. Earl can't do that. Didn't what happened in the hallway this afternoon—?"

"It's too late, Ken. We've had our chance—you've had your chance. It's too late to send you back to Manhattan tonight in this storm—doesn't that elegant little crate of yours even have a top you can raise on it? But tomorrow, after breakfast, you must leave. I don't even want to see you tomorrow."

"Chris—"

Whatever Ken was going to say, though, was drowned out by a thunderclap and a lightning strike and crashing sound very near to the house. As the sound from that was rolling away, the cook bustled back into the room with dessert. The lights flickered for a moment, but the electricity held.

After a strained silence while the two drank their coffee, Chris rose from his chair, said "goodnight" and left Ken alone at the table.

Later in the night, the storm having passed by, Ken sat, just in a dressing gown, in a Chippendale wing chair next to a fireplace set with gas logs that provided a perpetual, almost convincing fire. He was reading James Baldwin's recently released gay novel, *Giovanni's Room*, and absentmindedly playing with his cock—erect because of the subtext of what he was reading.

His door opened. Chris was in the doorway, also only in a dressing gown, which fell to the floor just inside the doorway.

Ken gasped and swallowed air. "God, your body is even more beautiful than it was before. I knew you couldn't—"

"Don't speak. Don't say a word, or, I swear, I'll be out of here in a flash."

Ken barely had the opportunity to lay the Baldwin book on the small table next to the wing chair before Chris was above him, encircling Ken's head with his arms, and bringing the older man's lips down to Chris' chest to provide nipple play. Chris positioned his hole on Ken's erect cockhead and slid down the pole. Then rising and falling, rising and falling, as Ken groaned and sucked on a nipple.

Ken wasn't one to give up control, though. He pushed Chris down on the thick-pile rug in front of the hearth, bringing the pillow he'd had at his back in the wing chair with him. He stuffed the pillow under the small of

Chris' back, which lifted Chris' pelvis. Chris lay there, legs spread and bent, his feet flat on the rug, as Ken knelt between the younger man's thighs, and entered his ass in one long, to-the-hilt slide. Chris winced at the invasion and total possession, but he fought hard not to cry out, to contain himself to groans, grunts, and low moans. No sighing, he screamed to himself in his mind, although he was totally lost to having Ken's cock inside him again.

Chris raised his arms, clutching Ken's biceps, and Ken grabbed Chris' slim waist with his hands. He fucked Chris in long, slow, deep strokes, with occasional visits to Chris' lips and nipples with his mouth. If he caught the dullness in Chris' eyes or the quiet surrender of Chris' body, he revealed nothing in the discovery.

With a shudder, he collapsed on top of Chris and started the series of spurts of cum deep inside Chris that the younger man remembered so well. Chris raked his fingernails over Ken's shoulder blades and jerked each time he felt the release of seed—once, twice, thrice, four times—in the only indication that he was part of the fuck.

He knew Ken well, though—oh so well. And, sure enough, after a brief period of hand work from Ken and kisses initiated and controlled by Ken as they lay there, plastered to each other's breasts, Ken turned Chris over on his belly, mounted his ass, and drove, harder this time, to another ejaculation.

In neither case had Chris himself come—just as in the afternoon. It had been really tough for him to hold off, but he had managed it.

At the door, as Chris was pulling the dressing gown around his shoulders again, Ken spoke for the first time.

"I knew you'd come back to me."

"I haven't come back to you, Ken. That was a no-regrets, no bad feelings good-bye. I still want you to leave after breakfast in the morning."

"You need it. You can't do without it," Ken spat back with a vehemence that suggested he hadn't been blind to Chris' placidity during the fucks. "You wouldn't have come for it tonight if you didn't want it. And if you didn't want it from me. It's time for you to wake up, get off your high horse, and accept reality. Earl's almost dead. You need to move on."

Chris didn't respond. He just turned away and stood in the doorway for several seconds—long enough for Ken to feel the triumph of believing Chris would turn and come back to him. But then Chris was gone, racing back to his own room, needing badly to masturbate himself for relief from what had been, as he knew it would be, a really good fuck.

* * * *

Kenton Walsh's idea of breakfast was most other people's idea of lunch. He was surprised, but shouldn't have been, to find himself alone in the kitchen when he appeared for his first meal of the day. He'd already made a run at getting into the master bedroom to see just how sick Earl Youngblood was, but the nurse who answered his light knock at the door could have played as a linesman on a pro football team. She obviously had been told that access to Mr. Youngblood was taboo to the overnight guest.

There were muffins on the kitchen table and coffee warming in a coffee maker. The refrigerator revealed his choice of juices. As he ate, he schemed. He had almost had Chris last night. He, of course, had realized that the young man was purposely not ejaculating—and having a hard time not to. The message wasn't lost on Ken. But if he'd had just one more go at him, he was sure Chris would have folded. Chris had let him fuck him yesterday. He just needed to give up the fight. Ken had won him from Earl Youngblood

22

when Youngblood was strong and vigorous. Ken could win Chris when the old man was on his death bed.

Where was Chris going to go when the old man died? Ken wanted to make sure that it was to him. He had miscalculated by not keeping the young man with him three years earlier. But Ken was four years wiser now.

After he'd finished his breakfast, he decided to find Chris. The young man had said he didn't want to see Ken today before he left. To Ken that meant Chris was vulnerable to him and knew he was vulnerable. It had been dead easy in the shadowed hallway when he'd first arrived. Chris couldn't be getting what he needed. Chris wouldn't have come back to him last night if anyone else was taking care of him. If Ken could track him down, he could put him in that vulnerable position again.

When Ken stepped out onto the front portico, he saw what had been the result of the lightning strike close to the house the night before. A large, old oak tree over by the garages and other outbuildings had been struck and split right down the middle. It was likely that Chris was over in that direction, inspecting the damage if he wasn't in the house.

Ken drew near to the tree without seeing Chris in the vicinity. But he heard him. Chris was very vocal normally during sex. There was little doubt that Chris was having sex somewhere nearby. But who in the hell with, Ken wondered as he sought the origin of the sounds of taking. He already felt deflated. He had been sure that Chris wasn't getting any. He had been counting on that.

He saw them through the window of a garden shed—a very well-appointed one, with shelves and counters and probably everything the garden crew of a large Long Island estate needed.

Chris was naked, on the small of his back at the edge of a counter, across the room from the window Ken peered in. He was stiff-arming the palm of one hand into the surface of the wooden counter to prop his torso up and the other hand was cupping the back of the neck of the older of the black gardeners. Thadeus, bare-chested, the fly of his work pants unzipped, his torso heavily muscled and glistening with sweat, was fisting Chris' left ankle, holding the leg of the still-limber dancer up his torso, with the ankle on Thadeus' shoulder. He was concentrating hard, with a fist around the root of his big, hard cock, to get the shaft deeper in Chris' channel.

Jeremiah, the son, was standing on the other side of Chris, holding Chris' other leg up and spread wide. Jeremiah too was stripped to the waist—and further—as the open fly of his work trousers were flared wide and the trousers were riding very low on the young man's bulbous buttocks. His torso was even more muscular than his father's was, and the cock jutting out of his groin in an upward curve that he was holding in his hand and stroking was longer and much thicker than the father's.

Ken had arrived in time to see the father turn in between Chris' wide-stretched thighs, take his hand away from the root of his half-lodged cock, grab Chris by the waist, and slam the cock home to the root. Chris' hand fell away from the back of Thadeus' neck and he was propped up on both elbows, his back arched, his head thrown back. Thadeus' head dipped down to Chris' chest and his teeth latched onto a nipple. Chris roared his surrender to the cock to the ceiling of the shed while Thadeus pumped him slow and deep. Ken couldn't take his eyes off the action.

The cock head came to the surface of the hole, Thadeus jerked and grunted, and his white cum creamed Chris' crack and dribbled down the young man's thighs. The cock went back in for several more strokes, and then the father was relinquishing position to the son.

Thadeus dropped back a couple of steps, and Jeremiah moved into position, taking Chris' legs and running them up his muscular chest. Chris lay his torso

24

prone on the countertop, an arm thrown over his face, and moaned deeply. The bigger, thicker cock slid in through the added lubricant Thadeus' prodigious cum had provided. The big black set his muscular legs, encircled Chris' slim waist with his bulging arms, and started pistoning Chris' channel hard and fast in long, strong, deep strokes.

Chris' body was bouncing up and down on the table with the strength of the thrusts. His arms went over his head, grabbing for anything that would steady him against the assault. His eyes were slitted and had a wild aspect to them. Ken realized that Chris was looking directly at him.

Chris knew he was there—he possibly even had assumed that Ken would be there and wanted Ken to see what was happening in the garden shed.

There went Ken's theory. Chris wasn't being deprived of sex. The black gardeners were probably servicing the little slut twice a day.

He didn't wait for Jeremiah's finish. He'd read the trashy novels on the black stereotype. The father had spouted like Niagara Falls. The larger, more virile son, probably had the reserves of Victoria Falls in his nuts. Ken did know how much Chris liked to be filled to the brim with cum.

Quietly and resigned to at least temporary defeat, Ken returned to the house, packed his bags, and got on the road.

* * * *

The movie producer, Ted Atkins, was laying on his back in the center of the bed in the master bedroom of the Long Island estate, his head resting on one arm bent behind him, and smoking a cigarette with the other one. Straddling his hips, facing him, palms of his hands on Atkins' pecs, Chris was slowly riding Atkins' cock.

To Atkins this was just one of many auditions he gave. But he did like the way the young man rode him and he really liked the look of the man who once had been a lithe dancer and who had only improved his looks as he grew older with added mass. He was uncommonly handsome in the classic blond sense. Atkins was sure he could use him in one of several movie parts.

He was pleased enough with the sample that he stubbed out his cigarette in an ash tray on the night stand, pushed Chris over onto his side on the bed, lifted the young man's upper leg, zeroed in on the exposed puckered hole with his cock, and thrust inside. With a cry of welcome, Chris arched his back. Atkins' free arm snaked around Chris' neck, arching Chris back and pulling the young man's head close into Atkins' face. Atkins tongue fucked inside Chris' ear before latching on to an earlobe with his teeth, as, down below, he was thrusting, thrusting, thrusting.

Chris was sitting on the side of the bed, leaning over, and cleaning Atkins' cock with his mouth when he heard the honk of the car horn from the gravel drive of the turning circle below the windows of the bedroom.

"Expecting company?" Atkins asked, taking the cigarette out of his mouth and blowing a couple of very satisfied smoke rings toward the ceiling.

"No. I'm sure it's Kenton Walsh. But he wasn't invited." He rose from the bed and went to the window. "Yes, it's him." Ken's Jaguar was parked beside—and being overshadowed—by Atkins' red 1956 Cadillac Eldorado convertible. Ken was cantilevering his body out of his roadster without opening the door. He had turned and was examining the Eldorado, apparently trying to locate its owner in his mind. It wasn't really Earl Youngblood's style.

"I'll get rid of him."

"Quickly, please. I'm not finished with you." Atkins was playing with his cock which appeared to be on the rise again.

Atkins had come to Earl's funeral at Forest Lawn. So had Ken, but Ken had backed off when he saw Atkins take Chris in tow at the graveside after the ceremony.

Chris had wasted no time in asking for a part in one of the producer's coming films. He wanted to go to Hollywood. He grieved over Earl, of course, but there had been months of preparing for the inevitable. And the best he could do, he thought, was to forge ahead on setting up work. It wasn't really about ambition to become a movie star, he told himself.

Atkins had wasted even less time in telling Chris what he could do to be put in consideration for a Hollywood film.

"When can we arrange to meet?" Chris asked.

"I can come out to Long Island tomorrow," Atkins had said. Earl had just been buried. He'd been dead less than a week. But how often do chances to be in a Hollywood movie come along?

Chris met Ken at the front door. All he was wearing was a sashed robe. The shock of seeing him thus took Ken aback. But he looked around and spied the black gardeners at work mowing the vast front lawn in the distance. So, he hadn't interrupted anything between Chris and them.

"Yes, Ken? What do you want? We're in mourning here. Not receiving visitors."

"I thought you would need consolation."

"What I need is a bath. I was about to have one." He, in fact, did feel like he needed a shower. Atkins' cum was dribbling down his leg.

"Can I come in?"

"No, Ken. I'm mourning Earl. Perhaps we'll see each other in New York. But maybe not; I'm contemplating making another go at Hollywood."

"Ah," he said, now remembering where he'd seen the red Eldorado. At the funeral yesterday. He hadn't stayed around to see, but he bet Ted Atkins was the one who got into the car. Bastard couldn't even wait a day before zeroing in on Chris. It didn't occur to Ken, of course, that he hadn't waited any longer than that either.

"Where will you go now, though? Can you afford to get out to Hollywood on your own? I would take you."

"You told me that once before and didn't do it. And I'm quite well fixed to take care of myself now, thank you. Earl left everything to me. He had no natural heirs. He formally adopted me when I went back to him."

"I don't think you are doing that much mourning for him. I saw those two black studs working you over in that garden shed. You found a diversion even while Earl was on his death bed."

"Earl provided those two black studs," Chris said, his voice full of ice. "When he knew he was on the way out, he brought in Thadeus and Jeremiah to keep me satisfied. And I, in turn, kept Earl satisfied to the end. We cared for each other and took care of each other—something that you're incapable of doing. You have only taken care of yourself."

"Is Ted Atkins upstairs? Was he fucking you when I drove up."

"Yes, Ken. Ted Atkins was fucking me, and now I want to go back to bed so he can fuck me some more and so he'll give me parts in his movies. You had your chance. There are no second chances for you. I want to be in the movies. In getting that done a movie producer trumps a fading actor in every respect."

Chris turned and slammed the front door behind him.

Resigned again—if only temporarily again—Ken climbed back into his Jaguar and drove off. Ted Atkins fucked them and left them more often than not, he was thinking. He'd hang around. He'd get a second chance at Chris one of these days.

Chris returned to the bedroom to find Atkins, naked, sitting at the desk by the window. He was reading Chris' manuscript—the crumpled yellow, lined legal pads Chris was reviewing over and over again, tentatively titled *Danny's Choice*. No way he'd let the story be identified close enough to himself to be called *Christopher's Choice*.

"Hey, this stuff isn't half bad. In fact, it's real good," Atkins said. "It's about time to try an underground film like this. Time to rip society open on homosexuality. I might be able to film this, given the right investors. Might take a few years. Did you write this?"

Chris' heart was racing so much that he could do no more than mumble a "Yes, I wrote it." A second chance at Hollywood. Maybe this was his unexpected second chance at Hollywood.

"Come here," Atkins said with a low growl. Chris stepped over to him, and Atkins pulled the sash off the young man's robe and spread the robe apart. "Nice, very nice," he said. "I think we need to get you out to Hollywood."

"I would like that," Chris whispered.

"We'll get back to that," Atkins said in a gravelly voice. "Now, go down on your knees between my thighs. Finish cleaning my cock with your mouth. Then show me you can give a great blow job."

Danny's Story

I guess if I were asked when the turning point of my life was—or at least the initial one—I'd have to say it was when I was sixteen and the Broadway producer, Evan Yellen, called me down from the dance auditions for the musical *Finian's Rainbow*. The show had a quartet of male dancers, but one got too near the footlights in a rehearsal, fell off the stage, and broke his leg. They needed a fourth on short notice, and I was auditioning for the spot.

I should have gotten the job, I think. I was the best dancer there. I had been well trained from the time I could walk. I think the only reason I didn't get it was because I was only sixteen at the time—and because I didn't have a backer. My mother had gotten me a few spots, but not in anything like a Broadway musical. My mother was a dancer too—a showgirl at New York's Tropicana Club, which featured Latin music. She wasn't Latin, but my father was— a Cuban conga drummer who had been in high demand before the Tropicana Club opened and had helped my mother learn that music.

My father was dead when the Tropicana opened in 1945, but my mother was a good enough dancer to score a job there—largely, I think because of the club owners' respect for my father. He had been killed at the Anzio beach landing in Italy the year before the club opened.

Having been born in 1930, I was too young to go to World War II. I'm not sure my mother would have let me, in any event. She might have dressed me as a girl, as some mothers did to try to keep their sons from being taken in the army. I could have passed, I'm told, as I'm small and lithe, move like the dancer I am, and have sometimes been described more as pretty or beautiful than manly or handsome. I might have wanted to enlist, though, if I'd been old enough in time, because my mother was the classic stage mother, and there were times I would have liked to escape her clutches. But I was never given the opportunity to consider being anything but a dancer on stage.

When I hit sixteen, all of that changed. My mother was a war widow, and the soldiers who had survived were coming home. She was barely thirty-two, was favored with great bone structure, and used every trick in the book to look ten years younger. She was largely successful and landed a returning hard-bodied, sexually experienced soldier from a well-to-do, if not knock-down rich, New York family, who saw her on stage at the Tropicana and pursued her. The problem—beyond the man being possessive and short tempered as a result of having grown up quickly in the midst of fighting—was that he was the age my mother looked like—twenty-three. He wasn't about to be seen with a sixteen-year-old stepson. So I had to go.

My mother, who couldn't pass up the opportunity to land a hard-bodied, sexually experienced, well-to-do man nine years her junior this close to when she'd be too old to be limber enough to do the Salsa, turned on a dime. She went from stage mother to waving-good-bye mother in the time it took her to maneuver Manny down the aisle. I, of course, hadn't been invited to see that happen.

It's not that my mother entirely abandoned me; it's mostly that she wore dark glasses and kept her eyes darting around to check for watchers whenever we met at a café in secret. And, of course, she didn't tell Manny she still was in touch with me. She did what she could for me, though, with suggestions and references, as she could, and some cash here and there to help me with my rooming house bill. Unfortunately, she didn't know anyone high enough in the casting world to help me get a good Broadway musical gig.

It wasn't that unusual for guys my age to be out on their own and working in that era. So many young men had been killed in the war that there was a demand for workers, even if they were a bit young, and the theater world had long been open to younger actors, dancers, and stagehands. These young men just needed a little support to be able to hack it financially.

That's where Evan Yellen came in.

I had done my audition and was standing in the line of others who had done so—they made us watch the auditions of our competition, which is why I was sure I was the best dancer that day. One of the stage hands came to me in line and whispered that Mr. Yellen wanted to see me down in the theater seats. He said the name reverently, which helped me decide to follow him—that and, not knowing who Mr. Yellen was, I thought maybe he was the casting director.

Mr. Yellen turned out to be a tall, well-built man in his fifties. Very elegant looking as far as my peasant eyes could see and well dressed. What I remember most from that first meeting were his hands—his long, expressive fingers. The biggest reason I remember them is that he was a toucher, and I felt his hands on me as we talked. Not anywhere intimate, but really friendly regardless.

"I saw you dance up there," he said when I reached him. He was standing in the aisle at the edge of where the lights from the stage extended into the auditorium. The audience area was in the dark. This was an audition. Only the stage needed to be lit—and the first couple of rows, where the casting people sat. He wasn't sitting there, or paying attention to the guy dancing now, so I concluded that he couldn't help me get the spot.

"You are very good. The best I've seen up there today."

"Thank you," I said. I was waiting for him to tell me who the hell he was and how much clout he had around here, but I guessed he must be important, because he seemed to expect me to know who he was.

"You won't get the part, though, you know?"

Like I hadn't gotten all of the other Broadway musical parts I'd auditioned for, I thought. Of course not. But I can't stop trying. "Why not, If I'm the best dancer up there?"

"For starters, how old are you? Thirteen? Fourteen?"

"I'm sixteen," I responded. I caught myself but too late. If he'd guessed sixteen, I would have told him eighteen.

"Still too young. The pity is that I see that you're ready, that the two extra years won't make you much better, because there's not much better you need to get."

"Thank you," I answered. But how does that help me, I wondered. Still, the compliment was nice. I was a little worried that he had his hand on my forearm, though. So far, I'd been pretty good at side-stepping the passes men were making at me. It was a real predatory jungle here in the New York theater district.

"Broadway is a dangerous place for young men under eighteen who look as good as you," he said.

I did a double take. Had he read my mind just now?

"Producers don't want any more trouble to avoid on the age issue then necessary, so they just avoid it. You might not get good dancing spots on Broadway until you're

33

eighteen. Maybe you don't want to hold out that long. Also, you won't get this spot because it's already taken."

"Already taken? Then why—?"

"They're just being careful, going through the motions, for appearances. For the unions and such. The dancer who will get the job is the third young man from the left in the line up there. He's twenty-one, which erases the age headache, and he's been fucked by the producer of *Finian's Rainbow*. Oh, I'm sorry. Did I disturb you with my bluntness or crass language?"

"No, sir. I know what being fucked means," I said through clinched teeth. And I knew what being fucked meant. This wasn't the first time I'd lost a spot to an inferior dancer who was being fucked by someone important. I was used to being fucked in another way by that. "But you said that I might not get good dancing spots on Broadway until I was eighteen, not that I could never hope too."

"It would be possible that you could get to the Broadway musical stage sooner—if you had a patron."

He still had a hand on my forearm, but now he had his other arm around my shoulder too. I was beginning to get the drift here. He wanted to fuck me. I'd fended this off already a couple of times, but I was getting tired of waiting until there'd be no complications. I didn't mind the getting fucked part, I didn't think. I had known I was gay for several years. And I knew that I was attracted to strong men who would work me. I just hadn't done it yet. I'd developed no interest in topping other men. But everyone I talked to told me to hold out until I was eighteen. Otherwise it could get very messy.

"You think that guy third from the left is going to get the spot—because the producer is fucking him?"

"I know he will. I know both the producer and him personally. I know the decision is made. I know the dancer extremely well."

"Extremely well? Meaning?"

"I was the first one to fuck him. I saw him when he was seventeen. I was the first one to fuck him—when he turned eighteen. He's going to get this spot in part because of a deal he made with me."

"Are you a Broadway producer too?" I asked.

"Yes, I am."

"And you're saying you want to fuck me? That you might get me a Broadway musical spot if I let you fuck me?"

"Has anyone been there before?"

"No. I've never been with a man."

"Would you be willing to go with a man sometime in the future?"

"That's the plan, yes."

"Well, then, yes, I want to fuck you, and I'll help you get dancing spots in Broadway musicals if you let me be the first one to do so. But I don't want to do it now—I'll help you now—but it would be on a contracted contingency. If you held off until you were eighteen and gave me your virginity and then gave me privileges as I wanted them, I will help you get on Broadway. If you signed the contract, though, and didn't remain a virgin until I fucked you, you'd have to pay a penalty—an amount that you'd have to work very hard to come up with. Am I being too blunt for you?"

"No," I answered, honestly. "It's refreshing to have someone be upfront on what they're offering. Not to mention that it's refreshing to be pitched by a man who is willing to give something in return."

He obviously felt sure of himself. The arm on my shoulder had dropped to my waist, and, in the next half minute went to cupping and slightly squeezing one of my butt cheeks. I was in the usual dancer's practice costume, a leotard, so there wasn't much mystery to him how well-rounded and firm my butt cheeks were. I was a seasoned dancer. Everything about me was firm.

"So, are you interested?"

"I don't know. I'll have to think about it. It's sort of a crazy offer, I'll have to tell you."

"I assure you that I can fuck you very expertly."

"It isn't that . . . it's just something to consider seriously."

"Are you perhaps remembering that you aren't a virgin? That your dance teacher screwed you when you were fourteen?"

"No, it's nothing like that," I answered. He showed his approval by squeezing my butt again.

"Here's my card, then. Give me a call. I can have the papers drawn up and you can come in and sign them."

And fuck me on the spot on your casting couch? I wondered. I looked at the card. It said "Evan Yellen, esq." and under that was "Broadway Producer." I ran my fingers over the print, half suspecting that the dude had cards in all sorts of professions, but I could tell expensive printing when I saw it.

The casting director was on stage and was about to address the line of dancers. I hotfooted it back up there in time to hear him say they'd made their decision.

"We have decided we want Aaron Feingold for the spot in the *Finian's Rainbow* men's dance quartet."

Feingold was the third guy from the left in the line. I turned and looked out into the dimly lit auditorium, but Yellen was gone.

After I'd had some time to stop seething, I went to a pay phone and called Yellen. He wasn't in the office yet, but I left a message agreeing to his contract. I had a failed audition the next day again, and he sent a car for me there. He got me in as a dancer in the opening of the Broadway musical *Brigadoon* later that year and in *Kiss Me, Kate* the next year, when I was seventeen.

A week after my eighteenth birthday, he sent a car for me again and I went to his office half way up the Empire State Building.

"I understand you had a birthday last week, Danny."

"Yes, sir, I did."

"Are you still a virgin?"

"Yes, sir."

"Do you remember that we have a contract?"

"Yes, sir."

"Will you please step over to that studio couch over there, strip off your trousers and your briefs, and go down on the couch on all fours—in the position of the dog? You do know what the bottom position of the dog is, don't you?"

"Yes, sir."

"And you do know that I'm going to fuck you now?"

"Yes, sir."

* * * *

"Just settle down and stop pushing at me, Danny. I'm in now."

He wasn't in as far as he was going to get, I was soon to learn. The pain was excruciating, not least because it was so strange compared to anything I'd experienced before. But I'd been assured that it would lessen and that, eventually, I usually wouldn't notice it much at all—not compared with the pleasure it would be giving me. And there was some of that already—pleasure. The expectation of it; the "it's finally happening" of it.

"Stop pushing on me. I'm in. You're fucked already. Got your cherry. No reason to fight it. Open to me and enjoy it. You're a dancer. Dance on the cock."

I was on all fours on the studio couch in his office— the proverbial casting couch—and he was standing behind

37

me, between my calves that jutted out over the end of the couch. I had twisted around and swung an arm behind me, the palm of my hand extending through his open and separated dress shirt and pushing at his muscular, hairy chest. I was bearing the weight of my twisted torso on a fist buried in the surface of the couch. He was crouched behind me, his hands gripping my hips, his dick inside me. Only a few inches, it turned out. He was going to be much deeper than that soon.

I know I was giving him a wild look. The look in his eyes was one of determination and of being a bit perturbed. I know I was crying out something, but I was trying my best that it not be a demand for him to stop. He wasn't raping me. I'd agreed to it—I'd agreed to it months earlier, in fact. It's just that now it was happening, it was overwhelming.

"Oh, for Christ sake," he growled. And I felt the hands leave my hips and he was twisting around to the nearby chair that he'd hung his coat over. The hands came back with a long, cashmere neck scarf, which he whipped over my head; pulling my wrists together, causing me to collapse my chest on the surface of the couch—my tail still in the air, still skewered by his dick—and tying my wrists together with it.

"That'll keep them out of the way," he muttered. The hands went back to my hips, grabbing, pinching. And that's when I discovered he'd lied about already being in—and already having been fucked, for that matter. All of my sensations went to my ass channel, which his dick was penetrating more deeply. God, it was big.

"You're going to split me!" I hadn't meant to cry out, but I hadn't been able to keep it in.

Soothing shushing. "It will take it; I won't split you. Open to me; you'll be fine."

"There, in to the root," I heard him whisper in my ear through heavy breathing. "When you learn to open to it

38

faster, there won't be this pain." And indeed, now that he was all in and had stopped pushing at me—and I began to relax, knowing that I wasn't resisting anything that hadn't already happened—the pain was a bit less. "Turn your head, look into the mirror over there. Here, I'll turn your ass a bit. Look at what's inside you. You can take it. You have taken it."

I moaned at the sight of how thick the root of his dick looked to be as reflected in the mirror, where just the base of it was visible in my hole. And my hole. Who would have known it would open that wide? I didn't find his "help" in showing that to me in the mirror reassuring. Well, not immediately, but there was a little thrill at having taken all of that. And that's as big as his dick would get—surely. But maybe it would get bigger while he fucked? I moaned again.

And the pain. When the hell does the pain lessen, I wondered as I moaned and groaned and voiced every variation of "ouch" and "oh, shit" that bubbled up to my lips. "Ouch" didn't express a fourth of the pain, though.

"So sweet, and fresh. I've wanted to do this for months. And so tight. I'm the first one, right? Tell me I'm the first one. I paid to be first."

"Yes," I answered through shallow pants and clinched teeth. "You're the first one."

He was. Would I be doing this if he didn't have something I wanted badly? I wanted a speaking part in the Broadway play he was producing to go on stage in 1964.

"Good boy." His hands were off my hips and gliding over my torso, patting and pinching. "Sleek young body—if I hadn't seen your birth certificate myself, I'd—"

My groan covered what he was saying. Not only had a hand found and encased my dick, but I also felt movement in the throbbing dick inside me—or at least I thought the dick was throbbing; I knew my channel walls were throbbing from the alien invasion. He was beginning to move the dick inside me. Drawing back, pushing in, drawing back, pushing in farther than he'd reached before.

"Take it, take it, take it." Each thrust punctuated with a command.

"Oh, shit, Oh Fuck! That hurts like hell!" All senses returning to my ass channel. What he'd done before tying my wrists together wasn't being fucked. *This* was being fucked! Pumping me as I writhed under him. His grip on one of my pecs and on my dick vice-like now. The grip eased and he was stroking me with his hand to the rhythm of his dick stroking my channel.

I shot out onto the nice red vinyl of his studio couch. "Good, good, come for me. Good," he growled. He let loose of my dick and lifted his hairy chest off my back. He had been holding me close and covering me.

Standing behind me now gave him more thrust leverage. He was pumping me hard and deep. I felt a hand running into the curls on my head, gripping my hair, jerking my head back toward him, arching my torso back in a tight bow.

And fucking, fucking, fucking. I was groaning and moaning to match his grunts and crying out who knows what. At that stage it must have been variations of "too much" and "please stop." But he didn't stop right away; he was too taken up with enjoying the ass of a young dancer-would-be-actor being fucked for the first time.

He did start to calm down and slow down after a short while, and he lowered his chest on my back again, tickling my shoulder blades with the coarse, salt-and-pepper hair swirling on his chest, and whispered, "Sorry, you're just so sweet. Have trouble remembering it's your first time—and that you're eighteen. But I paid for this and you want even more from me. Say that I paid for this."

"You paid for this," I said, with a gasp. "But It hurts, it hurts," I whined softly. The reminder helped me focus. He'd paid for this and hadn't taken the privilege until I wanted more. He wasn't raping me.

"It's going to hurt the first couple of times. But it will get good for you. Just bear with me—and work on relaxing, opening. I know, maybe this would be better."

He was pulling out of me—such a relief—and carrying me over to an overstuffed chair in a dimly lit corner of his office half way up the Empire State Building. He sat in the chair and pulled me down into his lap. He started to pull my shirt up and off my back, encountered my bound wrists and took the time to unbind them and then rebind them with the scarf once I'd been stripped of the shirt. I was naked except for my socks, and he was still fully dressed except for his shirt gaping wide open and his dick jutting up out of his open fly. Somehow the discrepancy made me feel doubly vulnerable and this whole situation seem sordid.

I'm not being raped; I'm not being raped, I chanted in my mind. I want something he can give me badly enough to do this.

His fumbling with my shirt and the binding was a pause I probably didn't need. The fear of the first taking and what might yet be coming flowed back in.

Once my wrists were rebound, my arms went over his head, my wrists lodged behind his neck. "Run your legs up the back of the chair on either side of me," he commanded. "You're a dancer; you can do it."

When I'd done that, he lifted and spread my buttocks and speared my now-more-open ass entrance with the bulb of his dick. I panted hard as he pulled me down on the shaft, whispering all the time, "Breathe, breathe, relax, open to me, baby. You're doing fine. Oh sweet Jesus you are so nice. And I fucked you first."

I fought hard to relax, to open to him, discovering how I could do more of that, how I could relax my channel muscles and start letting the tension flow out of me. He was right. I had nothing to protect. I was fucked now. I had agreed to it.

He began to lift my torso and pull it back down, his shaft moving up and down inside me again. It was better than before. Still painful, but I was becoming more resigned to it, more aroused by what it was we were doing. Now even that I was naked and he was clothed was making me feel sexy.

"There, good. Better for you?"

"Yes," I answered in a small, labored voice. He continued for a while and I could hear his breathing becoming more ragged. If he'd just blow. There must be relief from this if he'd just fire his wad.

"Kiss my nips," I heard him say, and I pulled my face into his hairy chest and kissed one of his nipples after brushing the hair aside with my tongue. "Yes, lick them. The other one too." His shirt front was wide open, his muscular, hairy chest pushing out at me. "Bite them lightly. Oh, fuck. Yes, yes." They were engorged, hard. I felt him shudder. And maybe ejaculate? No, maybe not. Would I be able to tell when he had?

I lost contact with the nipples and was arching my back and crying out to the ceiling because he was slamming me up and down on his dick with the hands gripping my waist in response to my having fired up his arousal by following his commands.

This didn't last for long, though. He slowed down and dipped his face to my chest and did the same with my nipples that he had commanded me to do to his. "Perfection," he murmured. "Young, sleek body. Dancer's body. Just the right hard muscling. Nips are hard too. You like this."

And I did like it. For the first time, I was whispering, "Yes, yes, like that," and moaning a moan of pleasure. And I felt my ass muscles relax even more. He no longer was too taxing for me down there. He moved his face up to mine and took my mouth in a deep kiss. I sighed behind the possession and, involuntarily, my channel was coming to a life of its own, caressing the shaft inside it, my pelvis beginning to move, almost imperceptibly. Rising and falling on the dick, sliding up and down on it, caressing it. So this is what those I'd asked about sex meant on how glorious it could be to be fucked.

He broke from the kiss and gave a low laugh. "Yes, you want it now, don't you?"

"Yes, yes," I whispered. And I did want it.

"Fuck yourself. Move your feet down to where the arms of the chair meet the back. Use those feet for leverage. Fuck yourself on the cock."

I did so, and unless my sensations were deceiving me, he was going harder inside me, and throbbing harder too. So, he *could* get bigger during the fuck. And with my controlling the stroking, the pain was less, the pleasure more. More throbbing slide along undulating walls, as the fear and tension drained from the core of my body and I opened more to fit the shaft better.

We were both calling out variations of "Yes, yes, fuck me." I gave him my load again up his belly and heard him laugh and mutter something like "Oh to be young again." I kept sliding up and down on the shaft, pumping my knees and pushing off on the crease where the chair arms met its back, getting better at it and being more in tune with it with each stroke. He growled a "Got you interested now, don't I?" in a strangled voice, went rigid, and cried out a final, "Oh, Fuck!" I felt the entirely new, and not unpleasant, sensation of being creamed by his cum high up inside me.

Yes, I would know when he dropped his load inside me. And when I thought the spurt had ended, another one came. And then another one. He resumed the stroking, and the slide was looser, aided by the added lubricant. I experienced a flash of arousal. "Yes! Fuck me, fuck me. Harder, deeper."

But as if I now was too much into the coupling, he was slowing down, his dick losing its hardness—just when I could have been lifted to a new level of want. "No, no," I whined.

He laughed. "There will be more."

We held there, forehead to forehead, our eyes locked, while, panting shallowly, we cooled down. At length, he asked in a low voice, "So, it was good for you in the end, wasn't it? You can take it now? You want it, right? Because we're going to do this again."

"Now?" I asked in mixed fear and anticipation.

"In a bit. But soon. I promise. You get over these first couple of fucks and you'll want it bad and will have it good, very good."

"Yes, I want it again," I answered in a small voice. I wanted what I'd come for and been prepared to take this for, but I wasn't lying. I wanted him to fuck me again. I'd gotten over a barrier I'd worried about for months. I wanted it again, until I was comfortable with it—and then I wanted it again and again. He'd creamed me. Now I could really say I'd been fucked by a man. And now I'd have another skill to help me get what I wanted from men in power.

"Your choice, Danny. You want the part in the play or not? This, whenever I want it, if you do."

"Yes, I want the part."

His hands pulled my arms above my head, and he untied my wrists and let my arms fall to my sides. I became aware that I was near exhaustion. Letting my arms dangle at my sides, I arched my torso back, away from his chest, and let my head drop back. I could feel him going flaccid inside me. I no longer feared this dick of his. I wanted to feel it hard inside me again.

"Beautiful dancer's body," he murmured, and I felt his mouth return to one of my nipples. And then the other. Sucking.

"Fuck me. Please fuck me again," I whimpered.

"We'll get back to that. Now, go down on your knees between my thighs. Clean my cock with your mouth. Then start showing me how fast you can learn to give a great blow job."

* * * *

After an experience such as Evan Yellen gave me for a first taking—and the second and third before he let me out of his office—it would be reasonable to think that I shrank away from having sex with a man, but I wantonly went in the other direction. Within the next three days I'd been fucked by four men and had made my next late evening appointment to be with Yellen in his office. I would never have thought I could be so wildly after it and wanton, but I eventually learned I had help getting there and that it was all part of a big plan by Yellen to maneuver me to where he wanted me.

Of course he wasn't responsible for me wanting a lot of sex once that barrier had been crossed. He frequently told me later, though, that he had gauged me for one who would want it constantly, which was no small part of him being interested in me.

The first man was Sergei, the gnarled, but highly toned Prussian-strict dance master for the staging of *Kiss Me, Kate*. The dancers were practicing constantly to remain limber for the performances. We had our own dance studio, with floors that matched the somewhat springy and cantilevered surface of the raked stage itself and, all along one wall, a full-length mirror and a barre, the thick, wooden railing at chair-top height that dancers stretched out their legs on.

Sergei was an imposing and fearsome dance master. He no longer could dance himself. He nearly was crippled in his early sixties from too many years of springing off his knees and straining his muscles to the limit. As we practiced and did our stretches, he moved around the room, his cane tapping on the floor to tell us where he was if he wasn't barking out insults and commands to this dancer or that, which was most of the time. He was a tall man, and strongly built, his body on the thickish side, although one would be taxed to find fat on him. He still drove himself as mercilessly as he did his dancers.

I knew he fucked his dancers when he could—or whenever he demanded it; dancers felt too lucky to be under his tutelage to deny him sex—both men and women. I heard him remark more than once in my hearing that "to dance for me, I demand total control, and there is one sure way of showing that." He had sniffed around me and I'd been surprised that he hadn't demanded I give him his due as the dance master, but I had learned back when I'd been dancing in *Kiss Me, Kate* that there was a bubble around me. It was like everyone knew of my "saving it" contract with Evan Yellen and were just waiting for the fruit to drop off the tree, floating around me, giving me looks, talking in double entendres, but not reaching out to lay a hand on me.

Sergei had been like the rest, but I could tell that it was a strain for him. And, truth be known, if he had demanded sex from me, even though I was only seventeen when I started dancing in *Kiss Me, Kate*, I would have given it to him—just like other dancers wanting to work under him—if I didn't have the protection of Yellen's deal. I was not unaware, then, that my loss of virginity might well have come sooner than Yellen snatched it from me.

The day after Yellen had taken my virginity, though, it was like the restrictions had lifted for Sergei and other men. The men on the set who had previously teased me and flirted with me from afar were up closer, touching me and giving me sultry and lusty looks. Sergei was more direct.

We were doing our stretches on the barre after the evening's performance of *Kiss Me, Kate* and before dispersing. Sergei was moving behind us and barking orders, the last for the whole troupe being, "That is it for the night, boys and girls. You may go now . . . quietly . . . but for you, Danny. I wish to see you stretch that leg out further on the barre before you go."

Even as the last of the dancers was filing out he had come in close behind me, one hand on my lower belly and the other gliding down my left leg, which was raised and lying on the bar.

"The underside of your knee isn't touching the bar, Danny. That won't do. Why are you having trouble extending fully tonight? Are you stiff?"

Yes, I am stiff and ache all over, I wanted to scream. I have, just yesterday, been fucked hard—for the first time, and the second and third time, as well. My whole body is screaming from the experience. And, speaking of stiff, you randy old man, I can feel the stiffness of your dick at my back.

Just as the rest of us, Sergei, his leg muscles bulging and well defined, wore a skin-tight leotard in dance practice. Unlike the rest of us he wore no cup under it. He wanted his dancers to know he had a thick, if not overlong, cock— and that there was a thick Prince Albert ring in the head of it.

"Yes, I'm a little stiff tonight," I answered and then winced, as he put pressure on my knee, forcing the leg flatter on the barre.

"And yet there is something more fluid in your movements tonight, a maturity I haven't seen in you before. Like you have crossed some barbican in your life. Like you have finally let a man fuck you." From that moment, I understood that he knew Yellen had fucked me.

He was holding me close, breathing heavily in my ear. I looked into the mirror and saw his ruggedly featured Russian face looking into my face, a bit of a sneer and determination in his countenance. "That is it, isn't it? You have let a man fuck you. Evan Yellen has called in his contract on you, hasn't he?"

"Oh, god. How did you—?"

"Don't speak," he barked at me. "I will speak." I shrank into him and watched, in the mirror, his tongue rim my ear and then move inside the passage and flick. I moaned and the muscles of my body tensed.

"Relax, little one," he cooed in my ear. "I am going to fuck you now too. You know that I fuck all of my dancers, and now it seems I can fuck you too. Yellen has had you first, but there are always other firsts. Yellen doesn't have a thick ring in his cock, does he?"

I moaned again, and my muscles, which had been calming down, clutched again.

"I said relax," he barked. "It is done. I will fuck you now. No use fighting it." Although this normally would make me further tighten up, it didn't. I surrendered and, in doing so, was able to relax my muscles. "Da, very good," he whispered in my ear.

I both heard and felt the splitting of the seam of my leotard at the crack of my buttocks, and of Sergei's large, strong hand ripping the material away until it was in tatters lower on the thighs. I heard the waistband of my cup snap, and that fell to the floor. His hand was roughly grabbing and squeezing my balls and the base of my cock, which was engorging for him. I was panting hard. The hand that had been pressing down on the knee of the leg I still had on the barre moved to my throat and he held my head, face into the mirror, making me watch the lustful expression on his face as he ravished me.

His cock was free and beating against the small of my back as he roughly stroked my cock, making me

48

groan—and making me come quickly in his hand. He laughed and moved his hand to behind me, smearing the cum around and into my hole, pushing it inside me with a long, thick, strong finger. Fucking me with his finger, nearly as big, I felt, as Yellen's cock had been. I writhed under his grip, but had very little capability of doing so—certainly not of escaping from him. He found my prostate and worked that, hardening me up again and producing another, weaker, discharge of cum, which was transferred to my hole, although with several gobs of Sergei's spit.

Then, while maintaining his throat hold on me, he moved the cock head to my hole. The PA was so thick, as was his cock, that I couldn't see how he was going to get it in. But, strangely enough, I wanted him to get it in. And remembering the previous evening with Yellen and how much easier it was when I learned to release my entrance muscles and slacken my channel, I did so now.

"Open to me," he was commanding. "Ah, da, da. Very good. You want me to fuck you don't you?"

"Yes, fuck me!" I cried out, wanting to arch my back, but only being able to do so slightly in his tight embrace, as, preceded by the thick PA, he moved up inside me, held ever so slightly to allow me time to open more to him, and then started pumping.

The rest was as before as he built up to a release and gave me his cum—except that the rubbing of that PA on my channel walls was definitely another first for me. A glorious first.

After he had finished and was holding there, giving us both a chance to cool down before releasing me, I looked in the mirror to see one of the black stagehands I'd been watching admiringly, Jerome, standing in the doorway to the dance studio, bare-chested as the stagehands often were after hours when adjusting and repairing sets. His hand was on his crotch.

Jerome didn't let me leave the building. It was like "open season" was plastered across my forehead—and, of course, I later found out it was.

He was there near the stage door when I was dressed and ready to leave. And he wasn't alone. Buford was there too. Jerome was a young black, maybe four years older than I was. Buford was older, maybe early forties. Both were magnificent specimens, though, showing beefy torsos with bulging muscles. I'd watched them for months, being aroused by them, but not knowing, until after I was initiated the previous day, just how arousing they were. Plus, here in the post-WWII era there was the definite divide between the two races, with a good bit of fear on both sides. My wet dreams of the previous night were not of Evan Yellen, I now realized—they were of two magnificent blacks who had been teasing me with innuendo for some time.

Each taking a forearm, they hustled me into the stage workers' workroom just off the wings of the backstage. Buford pushed me over to a wooden work counter, cleared the space with a swing of his beefy arm, hoisted me onto my back on the counter and started scrabbling at my belt buckle.

I heard the door to the room slam and the lock turn, and then Jerome was there too.

I didn't have time to think. I don't know what I would have thought if I had had the time. This was all new to me. I was opening up—fast—to a life I'd thought about—dreamed about—for years. I'm sure that normally I'd have been well into the fuck scene by now. That had been arrested by Yellen's "hold off" contract. Now it seemed I was making up for lost time. And if I'd had time to think about it I'm not sure I would have thought anything in terms of "stop."

Many had been the nights, I now realized, I'd gone home from the theater and masturbated to the memory of watching the hunky Jerome and Buford—and other stage hands—working on repairing the sets after a performance, bare-chested and flexing their huge muscles. All those times I thought it was just a general image of hulky men doing not fully understood things with me—to me—that aroused me. After the previous night I now knew what a man would and could do with and to me, and my thoughts were turning to more specific men who could do this. Jerome and Buford were high on that list. Therefore, my resistance already was low.

With a moan I laid back on the work bench as Buford stripped off my trousers and briefs and Jerome pulled my T-shirt over my head.

All of the tension and reluctance and any sense of guilt or of resistance—or, for that matter, not wanting what they both seemed determined to do, I released them of all uncertainty or fear of my response. I parted my legs and rolled my buttocks up, toward the hulking Buford. I'd just been fucked by the dance master. I already was in the groove. My channel was open and squishy with cum.

"Yes, yes, fuck me, you big strapping studs. Fuck me hard, both of you. I've wanted you both to do that for months," I cried out.

Their faces split with big grins, they proceeded to do just that.

Naked now, on the small of my back at the edge of a counter, I was stiff-arming the palm of one hand into the surface of the wooden counter to prop my torso up and my hand was cupping the back of the neck of the older of the black stagehands, Buford, bare-chested, the fly of his work pants unzipped, his ebony torso heavily muscled and glistening with sweat. Buford, in turn, was fisting my left ankle, holding the limber dancer's leg up his torso with the ankle on his shoulder. I had gasped at the size of his cock—not just the look of it, but the feel of it when it was only partially in. Buford was concentrating hard with a fist around the root of the beast, to get the shaft deeper in my channel. Huffing and puffing, I was concentrating hard on making my channel walls yield to him. Sergei had just been in there; I hadn't closed up yet. But Buford wasn't Sergei. He was Sergei and a half.

Jerome, the younger stagehand, was standing on the other side of me, holding my other leg up and spread wide. Jerome's work trousers fly was open and the pants were flared wide at the waist and riding very low on the young man's bulbous buttocks. His torso was even more muscular than Buford's was and the cock, jutting out of his groin in an upward curve, that he was holding in his hand and stroking was longer and much thicker, if that was humanly possible, than Buford's.

Only half in, Buford muttered "Fuckin' shit, he's wide open."

"Told ya so," Jerome responded. "Saw Sergei screwin' 'em. Screwin' 'em real good."

"No use wastin' time then." Buford rolled me up on one hip, turned to the side between my wide-stretched thighs, took his hand away from the root of his half-lodged cock, grabbed me by the waist, and slammed the cock home to the root. I cried out to the ceiling, my hand fell away from the back of Buford's neck, and I propped my torso up on both elbows so that I could look down to see how much of him was in me.

All of it, my mind screamed. On, my god, *now* I'm fucked.

I arched my back, both my flexible spine and my head. Buford's head dipped down to my chest and his teeth latched onto a nipple. Buford started pumping, sliding in and out through the cum Sergei had already deposited there. I roared my surrender to the cock to the blank brick wall behind the workbench while the big black pumped me slow and deep. I knew in that instant that having a big black, no matter his age, working my channel with a giant cock was Nirvana.

The cock head came to the surface of my hole, Buford jerked and grunted, and his white cum creamed my crack and dribbled down my thighs. The cock went back in for several more strokes, and then the older stagehand was relinquishing position to the younger one.

Buford dropped back a couple of steps and Jerome moved into position, taking my legs and running them up his muscular chest.

"Hey, forgot to ask. This OK with you? Seen the way you been lookin' at me and Buford for a while, and word is out you're free game now."

A little late to ask was what flashed through my mind, but my moaned reply was, "Fuck me. Fuck me now."

Slipping down from my elbows as the young black stud pulled me to him with strong hands on my waist, I lay prone and shuddered in anticipation on the countertop, an arm thrown over my face, and moaning deeply. The bigger, thicker cock slid in through the added lubricant Buford's prodigious cum had provided. Still, I had to concentrate to open my channel further to the cock. Good thing the younger followed the older—and the older followed Sergei, I mused. What next? A telephone pole?

The big black set his muscular legs, encircled my slim waist with his bulging arms, and started pistoning my channel hard and fast in long, strong, deep strokes.

My body was bouncing up and down on the table with the strength of the thrusts. My arms went over my head, grabbing for anything that would steady me against the assault. My eyes were slitted and had, I knew, a wild aspect to them I'd never felt before. I looked over at Buford, waiting and watching, stroking his hard cock. I hiccupped and groaned at the realization that he wasn't finished with me.

And, indeed, he wasn't. When Jerome had given me his hot, full load—or, rather, loads—he stepped away from me, and Buford moved right back in. I arched my back and cried out as he thrust hard and deep, leaned over me with fists pressed into the workbench top on either side of my waist, set his legs for leverage, and, moving up to the balls of his feet, started giving it to me again in hard, deep strokes.

Laying there, panting, exhausted, but a silly grin on my face, I watched the glistening torso of Buford pull away, his hot cum running down my thighs, and the even more cut pecs of Jerome coming into my dull-eyed view. Lifting me and holding me in front of him as he sat on the counter and pulled me onto his lap, onto his cock. Lacing his legs in mine, encircling my waist with a strong arm. Lying back on the counter and taking me back with him, his feet rising to the edge of the counter, spread wide, raising and spreading my feet too—and rolling my buttocks up.

Buford appeared before me again.

"You had two at once before?" he asked.

I don't know how he could have interpreted my deep groan as a "yes," but they proceeded anyway.

Grabbing my ankles and raising and spreading my legs, taking them away from being entwined in Jerome's legs, he leaned into me with his forehead touching mine, his eyes boring into mine, his hard cock slowly working its way inside me, on top of Jerome's already-buried cock, my mouth slack in a silent scream, my eyes watering. The throbbing cock, pressed to another throbbing cock, slid through buckets of cum into my channel. Deep.

I could say I was conditioned now. I loved every cruel stroke of it from the hot black muscle studs. I also realized that sometimes in my fantasies, I had been doubled by two black studs.

* * * *

"You missed the matinee. Are you ill?"

"No, I'm fine. Just very tired this morning. But that's what alternate dancers are made for. It's the first performance I've missed. One of them will be thrilled. And I'm here for the evening performance." If it sounded like I was being defensive, I was. I was attracted to this man too, and didn't want him to know why I'd missed the matinee.

It was the day after the black stud stagehands had had their way with me in the stage workroom—or, rather, much later in the same day, as they had fucked me into the new day. They were both working nearby when one of the leads in the musical, Keith Winston, came up to talk to me. Keith had sought me out often in the last year, hovering around me, but, like all of the rest, respecting the barrier Even Yellen had established until I was eighteen. Buford and Jerome worked efficiently, but their eyes often strayed to me, confident, knowing, proud. I knew that anytime I stayed late at the theater I could have some black stud excitement.

"Well, that's good. You're looking good, I must say. Exceptionally good." He had a hand on my shoulder. He'd never touched me before.

I admit that he was looking good too. I was looking at all men with an assessing eye I hadn't been in touch with before Evan Yellen fucked my virginity out of me. Just two days ago, I told myself. Winston, a good half foot taller than I was, looked down into my face. His expression was inscrutable. But he was an actor; he could do that.

I could have picked Winston out in a line of actors as one who played a leading role. He'd always looked like the leading man, tall, well-built, elegantly thin, expensively dressed, and with those killer blue eyes, flashy white teeth, beach tan, and curly auburn hair. Mr. Self-Confidence himself. And he'd been one to buzz around me. But until now he hadn't laid a hand on me. Until now. As he talked in a low voice to me as we stood together at the edge of the flying curtains between the wings and the stage, where the director was talking through a couple of changes in the script with actors, for a scene Winston wasn't in, I felt the hand that had been on my shoulder stretch out to where he had the arm loosely around my shoulder.

"Seeing as how you are well, I wondered if you might like to have a drink with me tonight after the performance."

I knew for sure then. Evan Yellen had let the word out. He had lifted the restrictions. I don't know how he knew that I was horny as hell. And maybe he didn't. Maybe he just didn't enjoy me and had dropped both his interest and his shielding protection.

The drink—two drinks, actually, both strong—were at Winston's studio apartment in Manhattan. The one-room apartment wasn't large, but it was in a tony building that must have set him back a good many bucks. One wall was all window, looking out over a fascinating cityscape from a dazzling height. A large bed dominated the room, but there also was a sofa and a couple of club chairs facing the city view and backed by an efficient kitchen counter, an island with stools, and on the other side of the entrance hall from the kitchen alcove, a well-appointed bathroom.

I had barely finished my second drink, when, sitting close to me on the sofa with an arm around my shoulders, he turned my face to his for a kiss. I showed no hint of reluctance. In fact, I felt none. I knew what he wanted, and I was horny for it. He paused in the kisses long enough to pull my T-shirt over my head. He already had his shirt unbuttoned and spread, to show a finely developed chest. I'm sure his chest hairs had been trimmed for effect, the light matting swirling around his nipples and then cascading down his sternum and flat belly to disappear mysteriously under the waistband of his trousers. The effect was very nice.

The leaning kiss lingered as he slowly laid me down on the surface of the sofa with him on top of me. He was feasting on my nipples as I felt my belt buckle being undone, and my jeans being worked down my thighs. I heard the gasp when he discovered I wasn't wearing anything under the jeans. He'd slipped my socks off too. Our shoes had been left at the door, his on top of mine, which both amused and aroused me when he'd done that—I'm sure he was unthinkingly projecting ahead to his "plan." He had been nervously touching me—including brushes of my basket—and moving his hand away as if stung during the taxi drive to his apartment from the theater. He seemed to be forgetting that I wasn't some male whore he'd picked up while cruising. I had known better than he did that he was going to fuck me.

He coaxed my left leg up and between his left hip and the back of the sofa. He sat up off my torso then and looked down into my eyes, checking. Could he proceed or not?

He could . . . and did. He lifted my left leg and licked and kissed up it, bending the knee and sucking on my toes. Naked, engorging, I panted and moaned below him.

Another searching look. Yes, fine. This time I told him as well. "Yes."

He looked slightly surprised. All of this time of dancing around me, and here I was, saying yes to what he wanted to do to me. No reluctance. Although older, he was a hunk and a half. A real change from the black studs—and from Sergei and Yellen, for that matter—but worth the experience. Smooth and steamy at the same time. And hard. While he'd licked up my leg, he'd unzipped himself and taken his cock out. Not unusually thick or long by any means, but hard, standing right up from his trimmed bush. Wanting to be inside me. Me wanting it inside me too. his fly was spread enough for me to see that he had trimmed his pubes in a V pointing to the goods. Auburn and curly. I wasn't surprised how well groomed he was. He'd even shaved his balls.

"Can I jack you?" He whispered. "And then will you jack me?"

"You can do anything you want to me, as long as I can make tomorrow's performance," I answered. My mind flipped back to the previous night. As glorious as it was, the black stagehands had worked me over so much that I hadn't made the next performance.

He shuddered. "Oh, shit. Oh, fuckin' shit," he murmured, all signs of his Yale accent gone.

Leaving my leg raised between his shoulder and the back of the sofa, he lowered his face to my nipples and slowly worked his mouth down my torso, across my belly, into my shaved groin, opening up over my cock, and sinking on it. Raising up and sinking again. And again. I groaned, moving my left arm over my head and clutching the roll of the sofa arm on the reverse side. My other hand went to the back of his head. My right leg was draped over the front of the sofa, my foot extending to the floor. I dug the heel of that foot into the plush carpeting and used the leverage of that to move my pelvis so that I was face fucking him. He opened his mouth in a big O to let me fuck it loosely.

I warned him I was coming, but he didn't seem to care. When I did come, he took it in his mouth, moved up my body and gave me a cummy kiss. He continued moving, though, pulling my body up so that I was sitting, sideways, with my back to the arm of the sofa.

My turn.

His cock was at my face. Somehow he'd lost his trousers in the maneuver, but his shirt was still on his back, spread open. I opened my mouth to him, first, though, taking his balls into my mouth, sucking them, rolling them, distending them from his crotch—just to hear his deep moaning. I then ran my lips down the shaft of his cock and palmed his tight, rounded buttocks, while he face fucked me.

He didn't come then, though. He withdrew after a few minutes of sucking, reached for my right ankle and raised and spread my leg out over the carpet in front of the sofa, let his cock glide down my torso while he stuffed sofa pillows under the small of my back, rolling my buttocks up to the angle he wanted, and slid right into me—slowly, savoring the rippling of my channel muscles to pull him in and my tremble and long sigh. After the session I'd had with the big blacks, I hadn't closed up much. Plus, I was getting a quick course in how to control my sphincter and channel muscles.

His pumping continued to be slow to the end, waiting for my shudder when the bulb was just inside the entrance and then groaning with me during the long, slow slide back into the hilt. I let my nails scrape down his back to his buttocks on the slide in and then back up to under his shoulder blades on the long withdrawal. When he was finished inside me, he lay on top of me, while we both slowly recovered our breathing.

"That was so nice," he murmured. "You have such a great body. And you're a natural at it. And three days ago you were—"

"A virgin, yes. You're great for your age too," I whispered, realizing only too late what an insult that would be to an actor approaching the other side of the hilltop from his prime. But he took it well. I knew then that he wasn't finished with me. And I was right.

"Not too old to have it up, fucking you, in ten more minutes," he responded, a hint of laughter in his voice, telling me both that he forgave me and that he wanted me again. "Do you like it harder or like that?"

"Whatever you want."

"Can you spend the night?" The question was given tentatively, hopefully.

"If you want." Another first. Something more than "bang bang, thank you, boy; now get dressed and get out of here," which, more or less, Evan Yellen had said that first time. This man was a lover. My first one.

"I guess," I answered, looking over at the big bed that dominated the small studio apartment. I wondered how many other young men he'd asked this. But right now that didn't matter to me.

"You wouldn't get much sleep, I'm afraid."

"That's OK." It was more than OK. I'd already reached for his cock, feeling it rise in my hand, feeling my channel walls shimmering. They wanted company again. I was becoming such a slut for it.

He rose from the sofa and lifted me up and held me to his breast. I hooked my knees on his hips and encircled his neck with my arms.

He laid me down in a heap on the bed. "Do you know the doggy position?" he asked.

"Yes, but are you—?"

"Yes, I don't really need ten minutes this early in a fuck. I'm more than ready."

This early in a fuck, I thought with a moan, as I went onto all fours.

"What, you think I'm too old to fuck all night? Don't count on it."

He climbed up onto the bed, hunched over my hips, grabbed my waist between his hands, and slid into me.

Yes, he was fully hard again.

Putting his lips to my ear, he whispered, "You are so sweet. I'm going to be so good to you. We'll make sweet music together . . . all night long."

And, starting a slow, deep pump, he did just that. My first fully attentive lover.

* * * *

"So, did you enjoy Sergei and the two stagehands, Jerome and Buford?"

I looked up and across the desk sharply. Evan Yellen's face was showing a smirk.

"You knew. You probably even put them up to it." But he'd only named three. So, he must not know about Keith Winston. Should I tell him—throw that in his face? Not a chance.

"When I consider continuing with a young man—past that first time—I want them quickly seasoned. I can't think of anything more seasoning than big black cock to toughen up a new convert. I sensed in you a hunger for cock. Am I right?"

I didn't answer. I looked away from him to the window, where birds were flying by. We were in Evan's office half way up the Empire State Building.

"Yes, I think I'm right. I'm told you seemed particularly to like the black cock. Did you like the black cock?"

"Yes," I answered in a low voice.

"Discovered you really, really like big black cock, didn't you?"

"Yes," I repeated.

"And learning real fast too. They doubled you, I've been told. True?"

"Yes." What did it matter. My gaze turned to his wall of scripts. Still not making eye contact.

"And you loved it. I read you for being a real hungry bottom."

He waited for me to answer that, but I didn't. Yes, I loved it. Taxed me to the limit. Made me so I could hardly walk back to the rooming house. Kept me in bed through the matinee the next day. But, yes, goddamn it, I loved it.

"If you stay with me, of course, all of that has to stop—except for what I tell you you can have."

"Stay with you?" I turned my eyes to him then.

"Yes. Why do you think I had you come here today? Why do you think I've let you know that I've had men toughen you up and teach you fast how to give yourself to a man. I've got another proposition."

"A proposition?"

"Yes. It's really quite simple. You continue being available to me whenever I want you and I'll continue to get you spots in Broadway musical dancing ensembles and perhaps a small speaking role here and there. But I call the shots on who else can fuck you. There will, of course, be the occasional investor. But not unless I tell you you can."

"And if I—?"

"If you don't take the deal, it's so long and good luck from here. You are better able now to get your own parts by working for them on your back than you were before you met me, so it's still better than before you met me. But I won't lift a finger for you."

He had led me into a trap. My main question was whether I cared. I had sort of thought he'd continue fucking me anyway. I didn't know that he'd baldly state the conditions. But I'd told him years ago that I liked that about him.

"I can sweeten the pot. You've said before you wanted to be an actor too, not just a dancer. And I know you have a decent singing voice. While you're with me I'll pay for acting and voice lessons and make sure you get the best teachers."

I thought about that. "Can I think about it?" I asked.

"For an hour and fifteen minutes," he said.

"Why that amount of time?"

"Because I can sweeten the deal further. One of my 'OK, you can have him' stipulations will be the two black guys, Jerome and Buford. You can have them once a month while you're with me. Yes, I paid them to fuck you the other night."

"Uh," I said, flabbergasted and unable to think of anything better to say.

"And this can be the first month. They are outside, in reception. I have a meeting to go to for an hour. This will be a freebee while you think about it, but when I'm back, I want a decision."

He rose from the desk and shortly after he left the office, Jerome and Buford strutted in, all smiles. They were stripping their clothes as they advanced on me. They sandwiched me between them, standing and rocking back and forth, but only long enough for me to be stripped of my clothes and all of us to get hard.

Jerome sat on the edge of the studio couch, pulling me onto his lap and cock. Gripping my waist he bounced me up and down on his cock until we were both heated up real well. Then he was lying back on the couch, taking me with him, lacing his legs in mine and pulling my legs up and spread. Rolling my pelvis up. And Buford was working his knees in between our thighs.

I looked into the mirror across from the couch, seeing my tanned legs, but distinctly white in contrast to them, sticking up and out from the center, being held at the ankles by ebony hands, my hands palming muscular ebony shoulder blades, four beefy black legs between my thighs, two running down, leveraging off the floor as Jerome fucked up to me. The other two crouched between those legs running up to bulbous buttocks a slim waist and flaring up to the broad back, the butt cheeks constricting and expanding and thrusting forward and back. Me knowing they were driving another hard cock—Buford's—up into me. I shuddered and shot my load for the first time in that hour—but only for the first time.

* * * *

Sergei honored the new rules with a sour expression on his face and a tendency to criticize my positions more than he did any of the other dancers, even while we both knew I was the best male dancer in the troupe. When he didn't think I heard him, he was telling the other male dancers to look at my form and follow it. He had no real choice but to honor the rules, though. Keith Winston was less cooperative, and I had to use guile and persistence to keep his hands off me until Jerome and Buford—quite probably at the command of Even Yellen—took Keith off to the depths of the backstage area one day and he returned with a black eye from supposedly having tripped over a coil of thick roping in the dark.

The arrangement with Yellen was fine, for a year and a half. He could fuck nasty and had a fetish for bondage, but his demands in terms of frequency weren't particularly heavy. He certainly didn't leave me gasping for air and my channel twitching like Buford and Jerome did. And their monthly servicing was something I always looked forward to. The acting and vocal lessons he arranged for me—and paid for—were great and those alone justified the freedom of choice I had to turn over to him. I felt the lessons were strengthening my portfolio a hundredfold. But what they didn't do was help me to step up out of the dance troupe into acting roles on stage.

I found this curious. I should be getting speaking and singing parts now. I had it all. There were few three-talent young men not yet twenty in the business. With Evan Yellen's backing, I should be getting better roles.

I increasingly became suspicious, though, that it was because of Yellen that I wasn't getting better roles—that he was making sure I didn't so that he could keep me under his thumb. Despite this growing suspicion, I'd grown complacent. I was making enough money to move out of the rooming house and into a small apartment—a tiny apartment, one smaller than Keith Winston's and in a not-so-great neighborhood. Evan had made suggestions from time to time that I could move to his house. But it was out on Long Island. The commute would have killed me. And, besides, I was having this sinking feeling that I was doing just that—sinking into oblivion underneath Evan's thrusting and controlling body.

The breaking point didn't come until 1949, in the form of Todd Means. Todd reminded me a lot of myself when I was sixteen—although he was seventeen when he came to New York City, grabbing for the brass ring. He was young, naïve, small of stature, prettier than handsome, sultry sexy without meaning to be, and a good dancer. Not as good as I am—or even was when I was sixteen—certainly. But a good enough dancer to be in a troupe on stage.

The revelation came during the dance team auditions for *South Pacific*. *Kiss Me Kate* was still running, but I could see that the end of its stay on Broadway was coming. I needed to line something else up. *South Pacific*, which was to open in April in the Majestic Theater, was having great reviews from those actors and dancers looking ahead in the Broadway season and trying to snag the last casting call fills.

There were two spots open for male dancers who could sing as well. I wanted one of those spots. I went to Evan for help in getting it, but he shrugged and said that *South Pacific* was going to be a blockbuster show. He thought I was good enough and would say so if asked, but the casting decisions would be close hold. "No favoritism in this one, I think," he had said. "It might be more advantageous for you for me not to speak out at all. You have talent to carry you now."

Todd was auditioning early in the set; me later. He had auditioned and had looked good. His dancing was great, but his singing sounded only passable to me. I was just about to go into my own audition when I looked down into the hall, and there, in the aisle, about where the light from the stage sank into the dark of the back of the hall, stood Evan Yellen. And standing next to him, talking to him—was Todd.

After my audition I saw that Evan no longer was in the auditorium. I told myself that he had come to see my audition, which I thought was terrific. I think the casting staff thought it was very good too.

I got one of the spots. But Todd got the other spot. I thought at least three of the other guys gave stronger auditions then he did.

When I congratulated him, he thanked me, but innocently said, "I think the producer gave me a lot of help."

The producer of *South Pacific*, I asked, outrage starting to bubble up inside me in response to Evan's claim that there was no "in" campaigning attached to this casting.

"No, another producer. Mr. Yellen. Evan Yellen. He has agreed to help me."

I looked at him, thunderstruck. He was seventeen. He was almost identical to what I was at sixteen. There was only one reason in my mind that Evan Yellen would be taking the young man under his wing.

I went directly to Yellen's office and confronted him on the matter. "You got Todd Means the spot in *South Pacific*, didn't you?—after telling me there was no favoritism."

"You got the other spot, didn't you?"

"Yes, but I earned mine. I was the best one at the auditions."

"Humility was never your strong point, was it, Danny?"

"Fuck humility, Evan. You contracted with Means, didn't you? You're going to pop his cherry when he hits eighteen, aren't you?"

"My arrangement with you, Danny, doesn't include you passing on who I fuck and who I don't."

"Well, fuck you," I screamed, as I headed for the door.

"I've never asked anyone else to live with me, Danny," he called out as I passed through the door. "Just you."

I fumed in a bar for a couple of hours, until well after darkness had fallen. I should have been exuberant—I got the part in *South Pacific*. Not a speaking part, but a part including singing on top of the dance, and in another major musical. It was going to be a blockbuster. Everyone said so.

So, why did I feel so used and betrayed? Yellen was right. I never demanded the loyalty from him that I had agreed to give to him.

I drank one—or probably two—too many shots of bourbon and, in the late evening, found myself at Keith Winston's apartment door. He answered in just a robe, having been ready for bed. I took him to bed, laid him flat on his back, mounted his hips, slid down his pole, and rode him like a cowboy, swinging my arms and yodeling—the whole nine yards. He was startled, but he raised no objection.

When I was finished with my performance and dropped down beside him in exhaustion, he asked, "Does this mean you are finished with Evan Yellen?"

"I don't know what it means, Mr. Winston. I do know it means I have trouble holding my liquor."

"You can call me Keith," he said with a smile. "I think first names are proper after the fifth fuck. Of course, that's the first time you fucked me rather than me fucking you. Tell me. There's something wrong, isn't there?"

"There's nothing fuckin' wrong," I answered belligerently, and then I shot off the bed and into the bathroom. I went into the shower, without even closing the bathroom door, and turned the water on, full bore. I sank onto the floor of the shower under the pelting stream of water, rolled up into a ball, and started sobbing.

He came and stood, leaning against the frame, of the bathroom door. I glanced his way. So sexy for a man his age. He still could be a high-fashion male model. And, in fact, he did do sexy billboard work for men's clothes.

He stepped into the shower, pulled me up, and faced me to the wall. He was close behind me, kissing me on the neck and cooing into my ear, telling me everything was going to be fine. Running his hands up and down my body; palming my belly and pulling my pelvis out from the wall, my buttocks jutting out; and his free hand running into my crevice; pulling my butt cheeks apart; entering my ass, still open and lubed with his cum, with his middle finger; finding my prostate. Making me moan. Making me come against the tiled wall.

I raised my arms up the slippery tiles of the shower, pressed my cheek to the wall, and whimpered a, "Fuck me. Fuck me. Make me forget."

The entry of his cock was slow, sensual, bringing peace. He slow pumped me while palming my pecs and whispering endearments in my ear.

"Fuck me hard," I moaned. "I don't want to feel anything else but your cock working me hard."

Complying, Keith pulled out and turned me. I climbed his hips and threw my arms around his neck. I kissed him hard, biting his lip, sucking on his tongue, while he cupped my buttocks and spread them and thrust cruelly up into me as deep as he could, the thrust rubbing my back up and down the wet and soapy shower wall.

When he'd ejaculated, he let me slip down to the floor, and I took his cock in my mouth and cleaned it. He turned and left me on the floor of the shower—where he'd found me—when I released his shaft from my mouth.

When I had composed myself and dried off, I padded out to the room. He was standing at the window, back in his robe, and looking out on the city.

"In many ways, this city is the finest place to be on earth," he said, in an "almost absently" voice. "But it can eat a person up. It can be so cruel."

He turned and looked at me. "Is the city being cruel to you now, Danny?"

"I guess," I answered, not looking at him, standing there, naked, and looking down at the floor.

"You are so beautiful. I can't think of the city being cruel to you, Danny. It's all I can do not to rush over there and crush you, to try to meld you into me as close as possible."

I didn't respond.

"It's not the city being cruel to you, is it? It's Evan Yellen."

"Yes," I answered in a small voice.

"Because of Todd Means?"

I looked up sharply then. "What do you know about Todd Means?"

"I know he has a contract with Yellen—just as you did. He has to remain celibate until he's eighteen and then he has to give his virginity to Yellen."

"How do you know this? Have you tried to fuck Means?"

"Yes, of course I have, and that's when he told me of the arrangement. You found out, didn't you?"

"Yes."

"He's not the only one in the last year and a half, Danny. I'll bet Yellen notches his belt with a virgin every other month—all built on contracts to help their careers. And he may have helped your career, Danny, but only up to a point. I bet I'm right on that. He can't have you become too much of a success—probably not as much of a success as your talent and training justify."

I said nothing, trying hard not to cry. Why in the shit did I care what Yellen did? Stability, I guess. He was my rock—or my pile of sand, I guess.

"Stay with me, Danny. You have so much talent. I have a movie role budding out in Hollywood. Stay with me. I'll take you to Hollywood when I go. We'll get you into movies out there. You'll be a star. Tell me that you'll stay with me."

Better than that, I showed him. I walked over to the bed, laid down with my butt on the edge, and raised and spread my legs. I watched him cross the room, a movement framed by my raised and spread legs. How many men had I done this for now?—raised and spread my legs. He shucked his robe as he walked. A beautiful body regardless of his age. His cock already proudly erect.

I turned my head toward the window, watching the city lights at night. He grasped my wrists, raising my arms over my head, slid inside me as I arched my back, and began to pump.

* * * *

Another year and a half. Thankfully the *South Pacific* run was a long one, because there was nothing else coming my way. Even the audition calls had dried up. I credited that to Evan Yellen, to vengeance.

Keith was a dud. He kept talking about his movie role in Hollywood and saying we were on the cusp of going out there—so I didn't need to worry about work and new roles on stage.

I became his maid and cook—and a hole to fuck every night. Sure, he was romantic about it and all, but he wasn't Jerome and Buford. He didn't have a big black cock. He didn't share me with others. There was a bit of variety, but it was all lovemaking. I needed a good rough fuck occasionally. I needed to be passed around as Yellen sometimes did. Even Evan gave me rough fucks—let me know I'd been fucked.

The apartment was much too small. It began to constrict on us. We fought. He told me we couldn't afford a bigger apartment—that I wasn't making enough, wasn't chipping in my part. I wasn't moving up the ladder. I scolded him about his promise to take me to Hollywood, to make me a movie star. He said "soon." I screamed that he had no balls, that his cock didn't satisfy me. That there were black stud stagehands in the theater who could satisfy me better than he could.

He stormed out of the apartment. But I knew he'd be back. It was his apartment. I packed the few things I had and left before he returned.

* * * *

"So, you want to come back to me."

I was sitting across the desk from Evan Yellen in his Empire State Building office.

"If you want me back. I'll even move into your Long Island home, if that's what you want."

"If you did that, I'd want you to stay there, to take care of me. To give up your stage career."

"I don't know. I guess. My so-called career isn't going anywhere."

"I would want you to stay away from Keith Winston. I knew he wasn't good for you. Too much a gentleman. No fire and a mean streak. You need to be manhandled and fucked hard regularly."

"I just feel so defeated."

"I'll keep you from that. I've never asked anyone to live with me before. You're the one. I'll be good to you—in more ways than one. We were meant to be together."

"Yeah, I suppose."

"You be good to me until the end and you'll be set up. You're still young. There's time, time to make it in the business, with the right backing, including financial backing."

"I don't understand. What do you mean 'to the end'?"

He gave me a hard look. "You don't want to know. But I knew you'd come back to me. I was prepared for it."

"Oh, yeah, how?"

"Jerome and Buford. They no longer work in the theater. They're gardeners now. I hired them to work at the estate out on Long Island. If . . . no, when . . . you come out there to live and take care of me, they'll tend your garden whenever you want it. It's like I said years ago. You love big black cock. You know it and I know it. Now, go over to the couch, please. Strip off and bend over the couch."

He was reaching into this drawer for the wrist and ankle restraints he liked to use.

I stood, turned, and started working my belt buckle as I moved to the studio couch. I couldn't help it, my channel muscles were twitching in anticipation of a good old rough bondage fuck.

* * * *

This is the story of my life to age twenty-six, of the opportunities I had and the choices I made. I know I never could write it up to be published; Writing isn't my forte. I'm an acting, song, and dance man, although what I'd really like to happen to what I've written would be for it to be made into a classy-production art film, something to push the envelope in Hollywood.

Since I left New York, I've learned a lot about Hollywood, including the underbelly part of it where there are so many gay men in the business, all playing the game of putting gay subtext into movies that only they and their friends will understand. I would like this to become a whole film of that. I know it never will, though. It's about producers and casting couches and hard bargains for young men's tails—often for virgin tail. Producers aren't going to let this get on film. The best I think I could do if I could get someone to rewrite it for me is to get it into print, with my own money, if necessary.

What I've put in my journal is what happened to me; I wound up back with Evan. I survived it, although, within four years Evan was dead, taken by a series of strokes. He knew he had serious health problems when he made that last deal with me. I have to say, though, that he was good on his promise. We were good together for those four years. I even continued with the acting and singing lessons. Inherited everything of Evan's, including Jerome and Buford. Went to Hollywood on my own, and with my talent and financial backing—and willingness to open my legs on the casting couch—I made it to near the top. That wasn't unusual, I don't think. I think that's the story of lots of movie stars—you'll have to trust me on that.

I did see Keith Winston occasionally out there, but we kept our distance. How did he make it out there, to Hollywood? His anticipated call for a movie role in Hollywood came the week after we split up.

Make Me a Star

Hearing the click of the lock behind me in the sacristy was what I would identity as the "Go" square in the honest autobiography I probably could never dare write.

Before that, Father Timothy had been standing at the sink counter, drinking the last of the communion wine, while I, fulfilling my altar boy duties, washed and dried the chalices after the last service of the morning.

"Father," I had said, "do you know what last week was for me?"

"As I understand it, your papers removing your parents as your managers went through, Brent. I still am not sure that was the approach to take. Your parents have meant well. They have been trying to balance your acting career with having a normal life. You know that I have counseled—"

"More important than that, Father, I turned eighteen on Thursday."

I heard him take his breath in and start to breathe hard. "You know, Brent—"

"Father, I'm not wearing anything under this alb. I've been naked under this alb through the mass."

That's when I heard the click of the lock behind me in the sacristy. He came in behind then, an older, gray-haired man, but still handsome and wiry, and with strong arms. Father Timothy had never been one to be above honest physical labor. I knew he was still hard bodied. I also knew, though, that he could be gentle and wasn't oversized. I had researched well. There had been other altar boys before me. I had seen him with them; they had talked to me about him—he himself had talked to me in ways that told me that he ached for me but that it would go no further until I was of age. I had a plan—to start with someone sensitive and not too taxing.

"Brent." It was almost a pleading voice. I could feel his hot breath on my neck and his strong hands on my hips. I reached down and untied the sash around my waist and let it fall to the floor.

"Brent. You know how much . . ."

Yes, I knew how much he wanted me. I knew the looks he'd given me, the touching. And I knew I wasn't the only one, or even the fifth one.

"Don't talk, please. Just be gentle with me. I've never before . . ." I took one of his hands in mine and brought it up to my mouth and opened my lips to his middle finger. I heard him gasp.

"Oh my . . ." I knew it was a strain for him not to say the next word, just as I knew it must have been a lifetime struggle for him to maneuver between the values he espoused and the desires that plagued him—that, indeed, had probably led him into his profession.

He was trembling, but it didn't keep him from pulling his hand away from my mouth, to stand close behind me, keeping his chest plastered to my back as I leaned over the counter. I felt his hands on my hips outside the alb, bunching up the material to my waist. I heard him gasp when he found I hadn't been lying about being naked underneath. And then the hands were on my naked thighs, moving up my hips and waist—and up to covering my pecs. He was kissing the back of my neck. The hands went back to gliding over my naked torso—checking to make sure that I was real and indeed naked—and I was finding the arousal that the hands of another could cause.

I'd never hardened up before without the work of my own hand. But I was hard now, and I felt as well as heard his intake of breath when he discovered that. Having touched me there with his hand and finding me in erection, he let his hand encircle it. His hand was trembling. I jutted my buttocks back into his crotch.

"Oh Sweet Jesus; oh sweet boy," he murmured, beyond control now. He slid down on his knees behind me and plastered his face to my crack. My arousal meter zoomed right up there, and I let out a long moan, moving a hand back to cup the back of his head, holding his head in close to me. At the same time, I widened my stance. That tongue in my crack was driving me crazy. So was the hand encasing my cock and slowly stroking it. Who knew there could be this much pleasure? I did know that there was to be pain too. At least at first. That was why I'd chosen him for my first. The others had told me that he wasn't so bad—that it was the younger Father Paul I didn't want to be my first.

I had to question them to discover they were talking in terms of size and vigor.

His hand released my cock, briefly, to cup my balls and weigh them and roll them together in his palm. Then it moved up to encase my cock again. I rocked back and forth and moaned. "God, God, God," I moaned, not feeling any restraint at all in my language. Farther Timothy was too occupied to care.

He hadn't given my cock more than four slow strokes after that when I tensed and couldn't hold it. I shot off against the counter cabinet doors.

"Oh God, sorry," I muttered. I was embarrassed, but this was why I was here, now. I wanted to get good at it. This was square "Go" for me. This was where I started learning to do it better.

"Oh, you sweet boy. If you—"

"Do it, father. Fuck me please. I want it."

"Oh, sweet Jesus. We will go to the rectory."

"No, here, now. Don't make me wait. I want to do it." What I meant was that I wanted to get the first time over. Then I'd work from there.

I heard the intake of his breath and he stood up behind me, his hands on my waist—on the skin of my waist, my alb bunched up on top of his hands. One of his hands was pulled away and I heard him struggling with the buttons of his cassock—there were thirty-three of them, I knew from having worked with the vestments. It took a while, all the time the hand on my waist holding me with a firm grip, as if I would have second thoughts and would slide away from him and escape.

I had no intention of doing that. I'd planned this for a long time. Still, I was panting and had to fight hard to keep the indecision from creeping in. I've done it already; I've had sex with a man already. I kept running this through my mind to maintain my resolve. There was no closing that door now. Another man—the priest—had jacked me off, such as it was. But that was sex with a man. And I'd get better at that. This was just the beginning.

It was his skin on me now. He was hard and was rubbing the underside of it on the small of my back. His hands ran up to covering my pecs again, holding me close into his body. He was kissing my neck again. I turned my head for my first kiss from a man. His eyes were a shade of gray. I'd never known that, had never been this close to him before. I could see the ache for me in his eyes.

I assumed this was the point that I showed him with my body that I wanted him. I certainly wanted him to do it and get it over with. I moaned and groaned for him and let my lips part to take in his tongue. I sucked on his tongue, thinking he'd think that was sexy. From his moan and the lurch of his cock at the small of my back, I decided I'd guessed rightly.

He moved his buttocks out, away from me, but immediately brought them back in, this time with his cock coming in lower, pressing into my crack.

I released his tongue and pulled away from his lips. "Oh, shit, shit. Fuck. Fuck me now," I growled. Yes, now, raced through my mind. Before I lose the resolve. Get on with it. I couldn't go anywhere, become a star, until I got through this first time—and through all the toning up of the act afterward.

He was looking around wildly and then I saw him reach for the bottle of scented oil we used for the candles on the altar. Right, I thought, I should have come prepared for that. He could be expected to do that.

The oil felt cool between my crack. Slick fingers were sliding into the crack and then probing me. I gave a grunt and muttered. "Gently, gently, please. Oh, God, be good to me."

He was becoming more frenetic, holding me closer, his grip stronger, his breathing heavier. He grabbed one of my wrists, wrenched my arm behind my back, and pushed my chest flat on the counter.

"Widen your legs," he demanded in a breathy voice.

I widened my stance and the shallow probing inside my ass went deeper. In and out. In and out. Was he fucking me already. No, it was just his fingers still. But then it wasn't. Something bulbous, throbbing, was at my entrance, insisting on entry.

"Open, open, open to me, dammit," he commanded. "Wider. Legs wider."

I opened my stance even wider and began huffing and puffing as I felt the invading staff moving up into my channel.

"Breathe. Breathe. Continue breathing. And open to it. Relax those muscles. Give it to me. Give it to me."

I was doing my best. I almost cried out for him to give me a break, this was my first time. God, did I feel stuffed. And the others had said he'd be easier to take than Father Paul? But I'd done it. He was inside me and I felt him relax a bit and that made me relax too. And it helped. I felt my walls loosening, accommodating to him. So, this was it. This was what being fucked by a man was like. Well, it wasn't so . . . "Oh, Fuck!"

That wasn't what it was like—not by a long shot. He began to pump me. Slowly at first but picking up rhythm and depth of thrusts. Panting hard—both of us. I writhed under him, which only seemed to hurt all the more and to take him in more deeply with each thrust. So, I settled down, tried to relax, and didn't fight it. He was in. There was pain, yes, but a hint of pleasure. And I had been told that the balance between pain and pleasure would even out more in the future. And it was done now. Just need refinements from here.

He didn't pump for long—that had been one of the advantages with Father Timothy that the others had told me about. Not particularly long and little stamina. I felt the creaming of my insides, which wasn't an unpleasant sensation, and then my senses broadened out. They had been concentrated on my channel, any pain anywhere else being dulled and becoming a distant second to what was happening inside my ass passage.

"Please. My arm. You're hurting me," I whispered, suddenly becoming aware of his strong grip on the arm he had pinned against my back.

"Sorry," he murmured. "Sorry about everything."

But he didn't seem at all sorry about anything. He wasn't finished yet. His hands grabbed up the folds of alb at my waist, pulled it over my head, and tossed it to the side. Once again he was running his hands all over my body.

"God, your body is beautiful Oh, to be young and perfection itself again," he murmured. He pulled me in close to his naked chest again, his hands palming my pecs, his face buried in my neck. He was going hard again—but not as hard as he'd been before. Still, though, he was trying to pump me again, and he was at least partially successful, producing a spurt of cum, which wasn't as full as his first effort, but that ended in a long sigh from him.

I felt his body relax more and then separate from mine. He pushed my chest down onto the countertop and his hands ran around to my back and caressed my shoulder blades. They moved down to the orbs of my buttocks and squeezed them. "Perfection itself. I couldn't help myself. Let me help you clean up and then—"

"Take me to the rectory now. Can we continue in the rectory?"

"You want to go to the rectory with me? To my bed?"

"Yes, please." I had to push this farther now that I had begun. I gritted my teeth, but manage a wan smile for him. "Can we do it again? I'm in my own apartment now—with other guys. No one is checking up on when I go home. This was my first time. I want to learn to do it better. Will you take care of me? I want more."

We were both naked in his Spartan bedroom at the rectory. The bed was just a double, but others had told me that had been big enough. He was at least fifty, but his body was hard. No fat. The muscles hard. His hair silver gray on his head, but more an auburn as it trailed down his belly and into his bush. The cock not terribly long or thick, but erect now again, as we had stood inside the doorway to his room and rocked against each other and kissed.

I sat down at the foot of the bed, opened my arms to him, and whispered. "Please, let me . . ." I drew him in to me with hands sliding around his narrow hips and cupping his thin, tight butt cheeks. He gasped as I opened my lips to his cock and pushed his uncut foreskin back to the base of the glans with my lips.

"Oh sweet boy," he whispered in exhaled breath, as he placed his hands on the back of my head.

I had no idea what I was doing—but I'd done some research, including watching a couple of porn films—well, more than a couple. But I needed to learn. I needn't be an expert with Father Timothy, though. I just needed to get it done and to have some experience to build on.

As I opened my mouth wider and then closed it over his shaft as I took more of him in, though, I sensed that what I was doing was already good enough.

He fucked me longer the next time, having regained another load, and both of us held it longer before ejaculating. This was the missionary position, I had learned in research. Me on the flat of my back at the edge of the foot of the bed, Father Timothy standing between and holding up my spread and raised legs as he pumped his cock in my channel. This time he had proper lube in his nightstand drawer, and the sliding was smoother, less painful. I controlled my own cock, too, and could back off when I was afraid I was ready to shoot, prolonging the time I spent in the "just about to come" zone. In his excitement, he had shot his load inside me in the sacristy. This time he tried to pull out before ejaculating, but just made it to my rim. I sat right up, though, having already come myself, pulling my legs around to hold him at the small of his back and clutching his shoulder blades in the palms of my hands.

"No, don't leave me, Daddy," I whispered. It wasn't lost on him that I hadn't said "Father," and it visibly pleased him that I was saying I wanted him inside me. He slid back in and resumed pumping, the cum mixed with the lube making for a very loose fuck that my walls were comfortable with. I was getting more than a hint of the pleasure that could be involved in the act.

He came again inside me—not in any great profusion, just like had happened in the sacristy. But he'd gone to the heights and had come again. I could feel in his trembling that this was new and special for him too. I hoped that this meant that I could be special to men in this way. I was banking on this being the talent to fulfill my ambitions.

We slept on the bed, next to each other, but not embracing too closely. He had been working my cock before he drifted off, and his hand lay loosely on my crotch. I heard a sound at the open door, a gaspy sort of sound. Looking up, I saw the younger priest, Father Paul, standing there—an expression on his face going from surprise and shock to interest to lust.

I pulled away from the sleeping form of Father Timothy and sat up on the bed, cross-legged and leaning my torso back supported on one arm planted behind me. I ran the hand of the other arm down my chest and encased my cock. I had practiced this pose before, not having any idea when or if I'd ever use it. But I was already a professional actor, in my own situation drama on TV. I had practiced a lot of contingency poses in my planning.

Father Paul was looking at me intently, his hands fisted up at his side, as if he knew what he wanted to do with them but was fighting for restraint.

"Yes, if you want me," I said in a low voice. "My eighteenth birthday was Thursday."

His fingers started to work those thirty-three buttons down the front of the cassock, and when he was done and had parted the sides and stripped off his boxers, it was my turn to gasp. As I had been told, he was twice the man that Father Timothy was. And his cock was standing straight up in a hard curve from his pubes.

"My room," he said. He held out one arm, and I rose off Father Timothy's bed and padded down the corridor toward the door at the end of the hall beside Father Paul, who had an arm possessively wrapped around my shoulders.

It was time to move up and to get all the experience and preparation I could. I was moving fast, but the faster the better. The movie I was shooting for was only in the planning stage. But who knew how early casting would be started?

I had known for some time what auditioning on the casting couch meant. I was prepared to give it a go now that I was of age and getting out from underneath my parents' management. I just needed the experience to make the most of the audition.

* * * *

"I hear that Ted Atkins is planning a movie on that controversial new book by the movie star, Christopher Wilson, *Danny's Choice*."

Grant Gideon, who played my father on the TV sit-drama, *Steamboat Landing*, turned his ruggedly handsome face to me and said, "Yes, I've heard the same. Hoping to play a stereotype—the conflicted gay boy in a world of social judgmentalism?"

We were taking a break off to the side of the *Steamboat Landing* set, as the scriptwriters fought over the wording of the day's shoot. As, like most soap operas in the early '60s, the program was filmed on the cheap, trying to get it good enough in the first take to air within the week. We actors laughed a lot at this daily dance of the scriptwriters. The actors did a lot of adlibbing on the fly, trying to keep a straight face while also trying to make the other actors break up from what the cameras and sound equipment couldn't pick up.

Grant Gideon had spent a lot of time with me in the last few months during these rest periods. I had a very good idea why, and Grant figured in my plans.

I also fully understood what Grant was saying about the role I played in this sit-drama. The industry was on the cusp of breaking through many taboos in American society. It was the early '60s, the beginning of the era of free love and "do what feels right" hippies. For years film moguls, for their own amusement and because actual life in Hollywood was a whole lot more open than across the rest of the country, had been weaving in sexual connotation subtext in their works. One of the more subtle of these was homosexuality, which was rampant in the movie city long before it could be talked about in general society.

One of the more popular homosexual themes was that of the love of an older man for a younger one— sometimes even a teenager.

The hint of gay interest—or at least confusion about his sexuality—was the role I had filled in *Steamboat Landing* for the two years of its run so far—the conflicted teenager in a family of three boys, all with different problems, with a father as a sole parent. The scriptwriters had had much fun slowly weaving the hint of confused preferences into my character in the developing (and interminably meandering) plot in a way that could be read and appreciated by those in the know but wouldn't normally be caught by the general audience that was still assiduously protecting itself from such evil doings. In recent weeks they'd gone as far as to hint to those looking for it a budding relationship between my character and Grant's that went beyond the fatherly.

Grant had discussed this development with me and, as a self-proclaimed method actor, had suggested that we practice how that could be subtly shown in the TV program. I wasn't born yesterday, though. I knew that he just wanted to fuck me. I'd been in his dressing room. He had my eighteenth birthday circled on his calendar.

84

The inside crowd in the Los Angeles film studios ate this multilevel writing on the edge stuff up.

I had been playing in *Steamboat Landing* for two years, since I was sixteen—playing a character perpetually two years younger than I was. In that time I had slowly caught on to the deeper meanings in the character I played. I would have been pretty dumb not to have. And I had two years to grow accustomed to that—to decide that I identified in real life with the character I was playing—and two years to think of how I could use that to get ahead in the film industry.

I listened to the gossip and heard the rumors. I knew which film stars had earned their rise in films by lying on their backs—and often with someone of the same sex. It didn't upset me or scare me. I could go with the flow.

My parents had been protecting me from that in my film career, or so they believed, but what I thought was that their protectiveness was what was keeping my career from taking off. And it was interfering with my developing natural inclinations. I didn't think they were stealing money from me or anything like that by closely managing me. I just didn't have the prejudices or scruples my parents did—and I wanted to increase the size of the letters in my name on the billboards faster. This was why I filed for—and obtained—my complete emancipation from my parents as my managers upon my eighteenth birth. It also was what had spurred a long-conceived plan to start to unfold.

The timing was crucial. The rumored film, *Danny's Choice*—one that purposely would challenge social and film industry standard codes—was the story of a young man coming into touch with his homosexuality and moving into that lifestyle. A story of being cultivated and initiated and completely dominated by an older man until a younger one came along offering him different choices and more independence.

The twist was that the young man found he couldn't manage to make his own choices and returned to his first, older lover's control. It would be an art film, not totally a pornographic one—it was the early '60s, after all. But there would be fondling, kissing, partial nudity and many not-so-subtle references. And some rumors said it would present the sex scenes graphically but artfully. There even were whispers that the actors wouldn't be faking the sex scenes, they'd actually be having sex—that maybe the most graphic parts would be edited out in a public version but included in an underground offering.

But everyone knows how gossips blow stuff like this out of proportion—not that I wasn't prepared to play the role however the director wanted it played.

The movie wouldn't play in mainline theaters and it wouldn't win any awards—in Europe perhaps, but not in the United States. But the star of that movie would be noticed and, if he played the role well, he'd rise to stardom—on word-of-mouth notoriety as much as anything else. That didn't bother me. Notoriety was one of the flashier forms of fame.

I was determined to land that lead role. I knew the emotions; I looked younger than I was. And I was determined to play the role well. My stint in *Steamboat Landing* would position me for consideration, if I could get the attention of the movie's casting chief and producer. Real life experience would inform a well-played role.

"Yes, I want the role of Danny in that movie," I answered Grant, looking directly into his face.

"And prepared to do anything to get it?" Grant asked.

"Just about anything."

"You realize that it will queer *Steamboat Landing*, don't you?"

"How so?" I didn't really care, but I might as well ask what his reasoning was on that.

"If you play an obvious queer on the big screen, the general public will realize that you're playing that in *Steamboat Landing* too. You'll kill the program. The censors will chop us to pieces."

"You don't see getting more than one more season out of this sinking ship anyway, do you?" I shot back. "The way the script is going."

"The way the script is going?"

"If you start fucking me off stage in the program, the general public is going to catch on anyway, won't they?"

I thought he was going to swallow his tongue before he managed to speak. "If I—?"

"If the writers add in hints of incest, don't you think that will tip the program over on its side? Don't you think the general public will start catching on to what's going on under the surface?"

"Oh, that. I suppose you're right. But you're willing to risk all of our cushy jobs here for a chance at a controversial art film?"

"Yes."

"Ambitious little prick, aren't you?" Grant said it with a smile. We bantered like this all the time, so I didn't take umbrage. It did sting a bit, though.

"What did you do to get roles, Grant?" I shot back. "The way I heard it you fucked a program director—a male program director." And the shot went home, which took more of the sting out of Grant's "prick" comment.

Our conversation paused, as it looked like the scriptwriters were about to descend to pass out lines. But it was a false alarm and we settled in with our coffee again. Grant settled rather closer to me than he'd been before and placed a hand on my thigh. If I called him on it, he'd probably just say it was part of his method acting thing. I didn't say anything, though, because it fit in with my plan.

"I hear that your documents dropping your parents as your managers went through," he said, seemingly changing the topic of the conversation, although I didn't see it as a change—and Grant didn't intend it as a change, either, I was sure.

"Yep, on my eighteenth birthday, three weeks ago."

"Eighteen," Grant said. "Yes, I have trouble thinking of you as that old. You play younger quite well in the program."

Trouble thinking of me as that old, I thought. Why do you have my eighteenth birthday circled on the calendar in your dressing room then?

Another pause, with Grant taking up the conversation again. "So you don't live with your parents anymore."

"No, I've got an apartment with a couple of other guys I went to high school with. They're doing college. I've got other fish to fry first."

"Is your apartment far from here?"

"Far enough. The bus is a pain. I'm just now looking for a car to buy. Think I'll get a Thunderbird."

"I just bought a brand-new Buick Convertible. A '64 Wildcat. Next year's models were introduced just a few weeks ago. I got the first one sold in Hollywood."

"Sweet. Sure would like a ride in one of those."

"I could give you a ride tonight." There was a pause; I sensed what was coming. I sensed he wanted to move that hand farther up my thigh—much farther. "I could give you a good ride," he added in a voice so low I suspected it was gauged to permit me to just pretend I didn't hear it, if I chose.

I didn't choose. We'd been bantering on the edge of this enough. He wanted to fuck me and I wanted the expanded experience in being fucked. I gave him a sharp look. We both knew we no longer were talking about driving in a car.

Time to play the wild card. "You want to ride me tonight? You want to fuck me tonight?" I covered his hand with mine and gave him a little "knowing" smile. There, he'd been circling around me for months.

Damn cocky actor. He didn't skip a beat or anything.

"Yeah, I'd like to fuck you tonight. You really are eighteen, aren't you? You aren't shitting me about that, are you? You really know that I can get you an interview with Ted Atkins for that *Danny's Choice* part, don't you? We both know that's why you've been sucking up to me for weeks. You know I've wanted to fuck you for the past two years, don't you?"

The lot Grant had bought up in the Hollywood Hills, overlooking the city, to build his house on wasn't on the way from the film studio to my apartment. But it was isolated, private, and had a great view from where Grant nosed the hood of the Wildcat to the edge of the drop off giving the big city panorama.

1964 Wildcats are roomy vehicles, and if they're convertibles, you don't even have to worry about headroom if the top's down. After Grant leaned over from the driver's seat, unzipped my trousers, and took my cock in his mouth—giving me an expert blow job that had me taking copious mental notes—Grant scooted over into the passenger seat, lifting my much slighter body, and sat me down on his hard cock.

I murmured, "Be good to me, but be gentle. I've never—"

"It's your first time?"

"Yes."

"Hot damn." Grant slowed down his approach. He was already buried in my ass, with me facing the dashboard, my arms folded on the dash and my head laying on my arms, but he held there and waited for me to accommodate to him.

I did the huffing and moaning and groaning that he thought would go with the first time—and I seemed to have been convincing enough with Grant, who was all kisses and thank yous and careful handling—at least until he got taken up in the heat of the moment. Early in the pumping, with me crouching up, leveraging on my feet, so that my ass was raised a bit from Grant's crotch and Grant could fuck up into my channel, I started to move my buttocks—back and forth and in a circular motion—just like Father Paul told me drove him wild. It got to Grant too. He lost his control and ended up grabbing my waist and slamming me up and down on his cock until we both had ejaculated.

I did what I thought was the appropriate screaming when being taken this way for the first time, and Grant had asked the right questions on stopping or slowing down—neither of which he could have or would have done—but I think I managed to make the right statements of wanting Grant's cock regardless.

Sitting, panting, side by side afterward, each of us with a hand on the cock of the other—both of us coming to life there again, Grant said, "You do that well for your first time."

"Thanks." What I was thinking, though, was that I'd had plenty of practice in a short time. It was Father Paul's favorite position. And Father Paul had become my favorite priest to practice with. I'm sure there are those who would wonder why I first gave myself to priests. The ways of priests weren't that great a secret, although the Catholic Church and society as a whole seemed to want to be blind to that—and probably would remain so into the next century. And, since I was reaching for public fame, a priest fucking me was likely to have too much to lose to call me out in public about that. He had more to lose than I did.

"I guess you want me to drive you home now," Grant continued. He wasn't hiding the disappointment very well that the session was coming to an end.

"If you get me an interview with Ted Atkins," I responded, "we can both get naked, you can lay down on the backseat, and I'll ride you into the sunset."

The backseat of a 1964 Buick Wildcat convertible is quite commodious indeed.

* * * *

On the following Friday, I rode Ted Atkins' cock in the producer's office after work hours, with Atkins sitting on the side of a studio couch and me in his lap, facing him, my arms thrown around Atkins' neck so that the producer could suck my nipples while I bounced up and down on his cock.

I couldn't play the "first time" role—Grant had gotten me the interview, and, I was quite sure told Atkins what I would do to get an audition—but I could, and did, play the "I've never had a cocking as good as this" role. I think I was pretty good at it. In fact, I think I'm a damn fine actor and deserve the role of Danny on those merits alone. But this is Hollywood. There's no straight road to anyplace worthwhile here.

Afterward, Atkins said. "You interview very well, young man. Very convincing. It's an iffy movie, though. So much depends on the investors. I have investors really hot to get a movie like *Danny's Choice* filmed. But the leading role in such a movie is all important to men like this. They have to know who they're dealing with. But, say, there's an investors' meeting at my house on Tuesday. Perhaps—"

I hesitated slightly. I'd been hearing rumors that the investors for this movie were no more than a chummy men's club chasing free-use young male tail—that there was no such movie in the offing. But I had to take the risk.

"I can be there. You'll put in a good word for me?"

"Well, I'm sure you'd be one of the leading possibilities."

"Take me home with you tonight. Let me convince you." My research had told me that Ted Atkins lived alone and was between personal trainers.

When I arrived at the investors' meeting at Atkins' Beverly Hills mansion on Tuesday evening, I made the trip by descending the stairs from Atkins' bedroom where I'd been—on Atkins' bed with my legs open—the better part of the days since Friday in Atkins' office.

As I came down the stairs, I saw them—seven middle-aged men, sitting in a semicircle in Atkins' living room. Sixteen wide-open eyes, including those of Atkins, followed my descent. In anticipation of exactly what I found, I was stark naked.

Damn. My descent was arrested by noticing that, though, all eyes were on me, some hands were otherwise engaged. Anthony. The little Italian dancer, Anthony—the same age as me, hitting Los Angeles at the same time as me, answering the same casting calls as me—was already ahead of me here. Leave it to Atkins to be making this a competition.

Anthony was down to his briefs—although that didn't mean much, because a hand was doing a disappearing act under the waistband of Anthony's briefs—and the Italian's lithe little body was wedged between two of the investors. His legs were spread, one slung over one guy's lap and the other over the thigh of the guy on the other side of him. The investors' arms had him in a close hold and their hands were everywhere on his body. Anthony was showing a scared expression, but I assumed that that was pretense—that he wanted the lead role in *Danny's Choice* as much as I did.

OK, battle on, I thought as I continued down the stairs. How will it be; how will I take them? I asked myself. Left to right or right to left?

Anthony's Choice

"Uh, Manuel. Please. We can't."

"You are a tease, Anthony. I am becoming weary of it."

The slim dancer rolled out from underneath the larger, muscular Cuban, who sat up on the bed and snorted his frustration. The two had been in a sixty-nine position on the bed, the dark-skinned Cuban on his elbows and knees suspended over the dark-complexioned, smaller man with the sultry, almost pretty face, and the black curly hair. Nonetheless, as a background dancer in movie musicals, he was as hard bodied as the muscular Cuban and could crack walnuts with his thighs.

The two had been stretched out in reverse and sucking cock. Manuel had also let his fingers wander into Anthony's crack, with his middle finger toying with the rim—which Anthony had moaned for but not objected to—and from there tapping on the hole itself and starting to sink in. That had moved into taboo territory. Manuel didn't force the issue, but he did test it on occasion.

Anthony, whose pay was low despite having worked in movies since he was sixteen, had lived in Manuel's apartment since he had turned eighteen two months previously. As a saxophonist in background orchestras and at clubs, when he needed cash, Manuel was better off financially than Anthony was.

Manuel had taken Anthony in at a cut rate as a roommate because he wanted to fuck the luscious little dancer of Italian origin. He'd been working on doing that for the past two months. He wouldn't take the smaller man by force, though. It had to be Anthony's choice. Anthony had continually said it was what he wanted, but that it couldn't happen yet.

"Why?" Manuel asked out of frustration. "I can understand waiting until you're eighteen, but I didn't lay a hand on you until you were—I didn't take you in as a roommate until you were. I'm not doing anything more than you keep saying you want to do with me. You suck my cock and let me suck yours. You let me come in your mouth. Why don't you let me fuck your ass? Are you afraid of it? Am I too big for you?"

"Yes, of course I'm afraid of it. Of course it's big— it's huge," Anthony said, forcing a grin, trying to take the edge off Manuel's suppressed anger. "But that's not it. Just be patient. Probably just for a few more days."

"Patient for just a few more days. You can't do something today that you will be willing to do in a few days?" His eyes went to the nightstand and to the book laying there. "Say, this doesn't have anything to do with the interview you said you had tomorrow with that movie producer . . . what's his name . . . Atkins . . . Ted Atkins, would it?"

"Why do you ask?" The tone of Anthony's voice was suddenly defensive.

"You're reading this book—*Danny's Choice*. And I've heard Atkins is going to produce a movie on it. Jorge is composing a soundtrack score, on the hush hush, and is already lining up an orchestra. I said I'd play. But does this timing have anything to do with Atkins? I've heard about

94

him and his first-time fetish. How he collects young men's cherries. You're not saving yourself for him, are you?"

"That's a lot of questions, Manuel," Anthony said, but he was looking away from Manuel. He couldn't look the Cuban in the face.

"OK, let's count them off, then. And be truthful with me or you might find your suitcase out in the hallway. You've teased me long enough. Are you reading this book because you want to audition for a part in the movie? You know it's to be a graphic underground homo coming of age movie, don't you?"

"That still isn't one question."

"Answer them." It wasn't a request.

"Yes, I know what the screenplay will be about. And, yes, I want to audition for a part."

"With the producer himself? Aren't minor speaking roles worked out between central casting and your agent?"

"I'm not auditioning for just any role. I'm auditioning to be Danny."

"The lead?"

"Yes."

Manuel whistled. "That's quite a jump from the dance line. And you're going to try to get the part by letting the producer fuck you? To take your ass-channel virginity? Is that it? I can't fuck you in the ass until Ted Atkins has fucked you?"

"Yes, that's right. But it's more complicated than that."

"Sounds pretty complicated to me already. How much more complicated can it get?"

"Ted Atkins has already paid for my virginity. He did that two years ago. He just accepted that he couldn't cash in until I was eighteen. I had to promise to wait for him to exercise his option."

"Exercising an option on an ass? That doesn't sound just complicated. It sounds Byzantine. What did he pay for this privilege? Looking around at what you own in this apartment, I gotta say that you must have sold yourself cheap."

"Not cheap. If I reneged, I have no idea how I'd pay him back. When I came to Los Angeles, I couldn't find any jobs better than a restaurant dishwasher. And I had a talent, a skill for the entertainment industry. Do you have any idea how few male dancers there are compared to female ones?—I'm not talking about Chippendale pole dancers. Classically trained dancers to work the stage and in movie musicals." He didn't wait for Manuel to guess.

"Ted Atkins saw me at an audition. I didn't get that gig, but he made a deal with me. If I'd give him my virginity when I reached eighteen, he'd make sure I'd have work from then—when I was sixteen. He's been good at his word. I've had work."

"Not great work, and not work that advanced you."

"But work. I managed to stay in Hollywood and to feed myself—and to be in the movies and do some stage work too. I wouldn't even have an agent if Ted Atkins hadn't gotten one to take me on. I wouldn't have worked the last two years at what I wanted to do. I probably wouldn't even still be in Los Angeles."

"But your ass. You sold your ass."

"I am gay. I knew when I was sixteen I was gay. I've shown you I want male sex, haven't I? I just haven't done it all with you. That doesn't mean I don't want to or don't intend to. I'm not sure whether Mr. Atkins would be thrilled to know how much I've done with you. It's just for a couple of more days, I'm sure. I got the interview—for 6:00 p.m., when it would be just him at the office. He'll call in the chit, I know."

"I don't know."

"And, don't you see? I'm asking for more. I'm taking advantage of what he could—and probably will—demand to hit him up for the lead in *Danny's Choice*. If I can make him want me again and again, I maybe can parley this into my big chance."

"You might have to fuck a lot of toads. You might become Atkins' boy toy."

"If Mr. Atkins has a plucking off first timers fetish, I'll have to work hard to keep him wanting me. And if I can do that, I can work it to my advantage. A lot of the big names in Hollywood have done that to get to the top. And it's nothing to you; I'll be coming home to you. Fucking toads will be worth it if I can come home to you. Don't you have any idea how hard this holding off has been for me too? I want you to fuck me—to fuck me silly. But there's so much to lose by not waiting just a few days."

"I don't know if you have thought through how rough this can be for you." Manuel reached over to the nightstand, picked up the copy of *Danny's Choice*, opened to a passage he seemed to already know well, and began to read.

"You're going to split me!" I hadn't meant to cry out, but I hadn't been able to keep it in.

Soothing shushing. "It will take it; I won't split you. Open to me; you'll be fine."

"There, in to the root," I heard him whisper in my ear through heavy breathing. "When you learn to open to it faster, there won't be this pain." And indeed, now that he was all in and had stopped pushing at me—and I began to relax, knowing that I wasn't resisting anything that hadn't already happened—the pain was a bit less. "Turn your head, look into the mirror over there. Here, I'll turn your ass a bit. Look at what's inside you. You can take it. You have taken it."

I moaned at the sight of how thick the root of his dick looked to be as reflected in the mirror, where just the base of it was visible in my hole. And my hole. Who would have known it would open that wide? I didn't find his "help" in showing that to me in the mirror reassuring. Well, not immediately, but there was a little thrill of having taken all of that. And that's as big as his dick would get—surely. But maybe it would get bigger while he fucked? I moaned again.

And the pain. When the hell does the pain lessen, I wondered as I moaned and groaned and voiced every variation of "ouch" and "oh, shit" that bubbled up to my lips. "Ouch" didn't express a fourth of the pain, though.

"So sweet, and fresh. I've wanted to do this for months. And so tight. I'm the first one, right? Tell me I'm the first one. I paid to be first."

"Yes," I answered through shallow pants and clinched teeth. "You're the first one."

He was. Would I be doing this if he didn't have something I wanted badly? I wanted a speaking part in the Broadway play he was producing to go on stage in 1964.

"Good boy." His hands were off my hips and gliding over my torso, patting and pinching. "Sleek young body—if I hadn't seen your birth certificate myself, I'd—"

My groan covered what he was saying. Not only had a hand found and encased my dick, but I also felt movement in the throbbing dick inside me— or at least I thought the dick was throbbing; I knew my channel walls were throbbing from the alien invasion. He was beginning to move the dick inside me. Drawing back, pushing in, drawing back, pushing in farther than he'd reached before.

"Take it, take it, take it." Each thrust punctuated with a command.

"Oh, shit, Oh Fuck! That hurts like hell!"
All senses returning to my ass channel. What he'd
done before tying my wrists together wasn't being
fucked. This was being fucked! Pumping me as I
writhed under him. His grip on one of my pecs and
on my dick vice-like now. The grip eased and he was
stroking me with his hand to the rhythm of his dick
stroking my channel.

"Stop! Stop," Anthony cried out. He was writhing in Manuel's embrace, the arm of the Cuban encircling his shoulders and holding him close while using that hand to hold the book. The Cuban's other hand was stroking Anthony's cum-streaked cock, the young dancer having come sometime during the reading.

"It needn't be like that," Anthony whispered. "But we have to wait for whatever it is."

"If I can't do all I want to do to you right now, at least I can make what I can do real interesting."

"What do you mean . . . what are you doing? Oh shit." He was laughing as Manuel grabbed him—Anthony was no match for the big Cuban in strength—went up on his knees on the bed, upended Anthony, and pulled the smaller man into his body. Anthony was plastered to his torso upside down at the level where Manuel could take Anthony's cock in his mouth and vice versa. Anthony wrapped his arms around Manuel's thighs for stability, but he did a perfect straight-leg split with his legs above Manuel's head. The two resumed sucking each other off.

The dancer's limberness and dexterity had been a key factor in Manuel's campaign to land him. Manuel was intrigued with the male Kama Sutra. He had big plans for how to use Anthony's body.

* * * *

"Would you like a beer?"

The question had come as soon as Manuel walked in the door the next day—or, rather, night. He'd done a gig in a nightclub and it was 2:00 a.m.

"Thanks," he said as he reached out for the can. "You get out of bed to greet me?"

"No. I was waiting up for you." Anthony was dressed in a sashed robe. He went back to the kitchen island counter for his own beer—or rather hobbled a bit to the kitchen island counter. Manuel gave him a piercing stare.

"You OK? You're walking a little funny."

"I'll be OK."

"You interviewed with Atkins today, didn't you? He fucked the stuffing out of you, didn't he?"

Anthony looked away from Manuel. He was standing next to the kitchen island counter. "The important thing is that I'm no longer a virgin."

"Oh," Manuel said. He took a big swig of his beer.

Anthony set his beer can down on the island counter, pulled the sash of his robe off, shrugged his shoulders out of the robe, and let it fall to the floor. He was naked underneath.

"The important thing is that I'm not a virgin anymore," he repeated.

"But are you too fucked up to be fucked again today?"

"I don't want to give you a single excuse not to do what we've both wanted."

Manuel fucked him first at the end of the bed in a modified missionary position, crouched over Anthony's prone body, their foreheads touching, as Manuel said he wanted to see the expression in Anthony's eyes during everything Manuel did to his body. Anthony managed to hold his legs up and spread out on his own throughout the fuck.

They had been sitting on the side of the bed, kissing, Anthony trembling as Manuel held Anthony in a close embrace with an arm around his shoulders and ran his free hand over the young dancer's naked body.

"Be good to me," Anthony whispered.

"As good to you as Atkins was? Was Atkins good to you, Anthony?"

The book, *Danny's Choice*, was still on the nightstand, and, without waiting for Anthony to answer, Manuel reached over, picked it up, opened to a passage, and started to read.

> *He was pulling out of me—such a relief—and carrying me over to an overstuffed chair in a dimly lit corner of his office half way up the Empire State Building. He sat in the chair and pulled me down into his lap. He started to pull my shirt up and off my back, encountered my bound wrists, and took the time to unbind them and then rebind them with the scarf once I'd been stripped of the shirt. I was naked except for my socks, and he was still fully dressed except for his shirt gaping wide open and his dick jutting up out of his open fly. Somehow the discrepancy made me feel doubly vulnerable and this whole situation seem sordid.*
>
> *I'm not being raped; I'm not being raped, I chanted in my mind. I want something he can give me badly enough to do this.*
>
> *His fumbling with my shirt and the binding was a pause I probably didn't need. The fear of the first taking and what might yet to be flowed back in.*
>
> *Once my wrists were rebound, my arms went over his head, my wrists lodged behind his neck. "Run your legs up the back of the chair on either side of me," he commanded. "You're a dancer; you can do it."*

*When I'd done that, he lifted and spread my
buttocks and speared my now-more-open ass entrance
with the bulb of his dick. I panted hard as he pulled
me down on the shaft, whispering all the time,
"Breathe, breathe, relax, open to me, baby. You're
doing fine. Oh sweet Jesus you are so nice. And I
fucked you first."*

"No, it wasn't like that," Anthony murmured in a
voice edged by a sob, his hand closing the book Manuel
was reading from. "It was worse. And, yes, he says I have to
keep going back to him when he wants me. Make me forget
that, Manuel. Fuck me. Punish me for what I gave him and
wouldn't give you. You should have been the one to take
my virginity. You were so good about not forcing me. But
take whatever you want from me now. Fuck me."

"I was saving this for a special time," Manuel said, as
he laid the book back down on the nightstand and opened a
drawer. He took two black leather straps out of the drawer.
"Do you know what these are?"

"Yes, wrist restraints."

"Atkins bound you. Shall we take up where he left
off?"

Anthony licked his lips and whimpered.

He was on his back on the bed, his arms raised and
spread, his wrists bound to the headboard over his head.
Manuel was on his knees, between Anthony's legs, arched
over Anthony's torso, Anthony's thighs running up
Manuel's thighs, his knees hooked on Manuel's hips.

It started awkwardly with Anthony panting hard and
almost crying when Manuel had no more than his bulb
inside.

"Did he tear you up? Did that monster split you?"
Manuel growled.

"No, no. It's not that. You're bigger, so much bigger
than he was."

Manuel laughed. "In time I'll have your channel reamed to my size. We'll go slow this time, though."

And he did go slow, at least initially, at least until he was fully saddled and until he lost control in the heat of the pumping. By then, though, as painful as it was, Anthony was consumed by lust and, rocking back and forth on his shoulder blades and pulling at the restraints on his wrists. All of his screams were cries for "Yes, harder. Yes, deeper. Fuck me. Screw me. Punish me. Split me. Ream me out!"

Manuel got more inventive as the night went on. So much lust and frustration had built up that the virile Cuban stud fucked all night and into the morning. Though increasingly exhausted, Anthony stayed with him. The dam had burst. He could fuck whoever and however much he wanted to. And now he wanted everything Manuel could give him. The big Cuban was a cum factory, and each ejaculation made the slide easier. With each fuck, Anthony's channel walls were coaxed to stretch and loosen more. Anthony couldn't wait to be fitted for Manuel's cock to the point that the fucking would be all pleasure, no pain.

Taking Atkins the next time now would be a piece of cake.

They showered together after the first fuck, with Anthony thinking that was probably going to be it for the night. It already was nearly 3:00 a.m. It had taken some time for Anthony to take the whole cock, and once in and Anthony able to take the pumping, the virile stud pumped forever, Anthony coming and getting hard again before Manuel creamed him.

They had showered together and horsed around quite a bit. Coming out of the bathroom and toward the bed, Manuel grabbed Anthony from behind and pulled the dancer close into his body. He crouched down and commanded, "Jut your buttocks up and back at me." When Anthony did that, he immediately cried out, as a hard cock was moving up inside him. Manuel encircled Anthony's waist with one arm and lifted the dancer off the floor. Manuel's other hand palmed Anthony's throat and held Anthony's head into the hollow of his shoulder. Anthony was dangling in front of Manuel, embraced and immobilized while the Cuban fucked him.

Manuel didn't come in that position, though. When he came, he had reversed Anthony, the two face-to-face, with Manuel standing on the floor in a crouched position for balance, and Anthony's legs hooked on Manuel's hips, his wrists locked behind Manuel's neck, and Manuel's hips thrusting, thrusting, thrusting.

After he'd filled Anthony's ass with cum, he tossed the young dancer on the bed and came down beside him, flinging his arm over Anthony's chest. "Now I rest."

"You rest? What about me?"

"You can't take any more."

"I want more."

"That's not an answer to the question asked."

"I know."

"The interview today. Did you get the part?"

"I don't know. I have to meet with the investors."

"You have to fuck each one of them?"

"There's an investors' meeting I have to go to—at Atkins' house—next Tuesday."

"And you have to fuck all of them together."

"Don't be silly."

"I'm not being silly. If you've got to fuck that many toads, you'll need more practice."

"Manuel. Don't you think . . . Christ almighty you're hard again."

"And I'm a little tired, so this time you fuck me."

Manuel turned, lifted Anthony's body up, his biceps and pectorals bulging, and held Anthony over him, Anthony making his body go straight with his own strong muscle power, until Manuel was on his back.

"Sit on my cock facing my bent legs and hug the legs. On your knees, feet running back toward my shoulders. Yes, like that. Now fuck yourself on my cock." Half way through the fuck, Manuel wrapped his arms around Anthony's chest, pulling Anthony's shoulder blades back into his own pecs and jack knifing Anthony's bent legs to a degree that only a limber dancer could manage. He raised his own pelvis up, using his bent legs and feet planted firmly on the bed for leverage, and piston fucked up into Anthony's channel.

The fucking continued in intricate positions until daylight warmed the closed curtains on the window. Only then did Manuel turn onto his side away from Anthony's stretched and totally used body, and drift off into snoring.

Would it be like this every night? Anthony wondered before he too drifted off to sleep. Surely not. One part of him wanted it, but another screamed at him that he couldn't do this and be able to hold down a job at the same time. It was only because of the pent-up frustration of both of them from the last two months. Surely that was all it was. He allowed his eyes to shut.

When he opened them, he was on his belly, one arm and his head hanging over the side of the bed and the other arm flung out in the other direction. His ass was throbbing. It wasn't exactly a painful throb, but it definitely was a "Yes, I am here and I have been taken hard" throb. It felt like it had been expanded to the size of a subway tunnel— and, indeed, Manuel must have made great progress toward reaming it for his easy access. And it felt wet and sticky. It took him a few moments to realize he was alone on the bed.

He could hear humming from the bathroom. The door was open and he saw Manuel emerge. He was rubbing his hair with a towel and was naked. And in magnificent erection.

Oh, shit. Oh, fuck, he thought. Manuel must have heard the moan.

"You're awake."

"Yes. What's for breakfast." The stud surely must be starving. Maybe his mind could be diverted.

"Me, I'll have a slice of ass for breakfast." Manuel mounted the bed and then mounted Anthony's buttocks, driving his hard cock into the crack and slurping into the hole, which was open wide to him and was well- and naturally lubricated. He began to pump immediately.

"Oh, shit. Oh, fuck," Anthony murmured in surrender.

* * * *

Anthony looked up in surprise to see Brent Bradley, another actor he always seemed to be auditioning against, descend the stairs in Ted Atkins' Beverly Hills home. Brent was naked, leaving no doubt that he was there to compete with Anthony once again—for the lead part in *Danny's Choice*. And since he was coming down from the bedroom level rather than through the front door, as Anthony had done, Anthony got the impression that Brent already had an inside track on auditioning for the part.

To his credit, though, Brent looked equally startled to see that Anthony was there.

Manuel had been dead on right about fucking toads. Brent had arrived at Atkins' meeting of the investors, to find seven men sitting in a semicircle in the living room, all with slitted eyes, licking their lips, and moving a hand to their crotch when Anthony was ushered into the room by Atkins. The producer had already told Anthony in the foyer that, if he wanted the part in *Danny's Choice*, he'd have to impress the investors—and that the investors would let him know what would impress them.

106

Well, maybe "toad" didn't apply to all of them, Anthony thought. About half of them weren't too old and looked like they were in good shape. They all looked like predators, though.

When Brent descended the stairs, Anthony was already being shown what two of the investors thought might impress them. He had one on either side of him, close, on a sofa. They each had an arm around his back, with a beefy hand palming a pec. Anthony was stripped down to his briefs, although that didn't mean much, because one of the men had his hand down the front of Anthony's briefs and was exploring Anthony's cock and balls. The other one was gliding his hands over Anthony's torso and thighs. Anthony's legs were spread and draped over the thighs of the men on either side.

He only had time to watch Brent walk into a grouping of three men and be swallowed up as they each rose and seemed to crouch over him before the man who had been exploring his body with his hand decided that Anthony needed to turn onto a hip and move his legs together while the man who had been fondling his balls was pushing his briefs down his legs. The men were fully clothed, expect that their flies were open and their cocks were exposed. They both were in erection.

The "turn to the opposite hip" man took his arm away from around Anthony's shoulder and was working on pulling Anthony over onto his lap. The other man was pulling Anthony's briefs the rest of the way off his legs and sinking down between Anthony's thighs onto his knees.

Anthony gasped as the man who now was under him pulled Anthony's channel down on his cock and began to poke up into him. The man's arms had come up and around Anthony's torso and his hands were palming Anthony's pectorals. The man kneeling between his legs sucked his cock and rolled his balls in a grip that had Anthony's eyes watering.

107

He looked over to where Brent had sunk into the mire and viewed in blurry vision the legs of a dancer hooked on the meaty hips of a set of fat buttocks. The buttocks were tightening and loosening and moving forward and back in a steady rhythm. Another half-naked heavy-set man was at one side of Brent, holding Brent's arms up with a grip on his wrists. Just half of the profile of Brent's face could be seen pointed in the other direction. A third man, trouserless, his shirt unbuttoned all the way down the front and spread, was cupping Brent's head in his hands and guiding Brent's mouth on his cock. This was a younger man, in very good condition.

A third man had approached Anthony now. He also was younger, trouserless and half losing his shirt. And he also was trim and well muscled. He too had a big, erect cock. He climbed up with his bare feet on the sofa, a foot at each side of the thighs of the man who had Anthony in his lap. He crouched down to attain a good angle, fisted Anthony's hair in one hand to pull Anthony's face into position, and guided his dick into Anthony's mouth with the other hand.

Later, both Anthony and Brent were positioned cross-wise on a bed in an upstairs bedroom. Two of the more athletic investors were laying on the bed, legs stretching against each others, both propped up on their elbows and enjoying the view, as Brent, crouched over their nearly touching crotches, fisted their cocks together, sank his channel on the bundle, and started rising and falling on the bundled cocks.

Anthony was riding the cock of one of the heavier investors, the investor lying on his back, at the edge of the bed, his feet on the floor, and Anthony facing away from him and nestling his buttocks against the man's crotch. The man's cock was inside his channel. Anthony's feet also were on the floor and he was using them for leverage to rise and fall on the fat man's shaft—that is until one of the trimmer and better-muscled men kneed his way between the spread legs of Anthony and the man whose pole Anthony was riding. The more fit man reached down and grabbed Anthony's ankles and raised and spread Anthony's legs, causing Anthony to fall back onto the other man's chest and his buttocks to roll up.

The trim man's cock—it was the biggest Anthony saw in the group—moved to Anthony's hole right above the underside of the cock already inside the young dancer.

* * * *

Anthony and Manuel were on Manuel's bed, facing each other. Manuel's legs were stretched out in front of him under Anthony's buttocks. Anthony's buttocks were pulled up onto Manuel's thighs and his legs were wrapped around Manuel's hips. Anthony's torso was cantilevered back over Manuel's stretch legs, held there by Manuel's grip on his sides. Anthony's arms were dangling at his sides and his head was thrown back. Manuel had already fucked him in this position, filling him deep with cum. Anthony wanted a repeat in this position, and they were waiting for Manuel to harden up again, while Manuel whispered to his lover about all of the positions he intended to try in the next few hours.

Anthony groaned at the litany of all the ways he was going to be taken. But it had been a slow, peaceful fuck. He had thoroughly enjoyed it.

"Did the investors' meeting today go well?" Manuel asked. Once again, he'd had a band gig and didn't get home until after 2:00 a.m. They'd gone immediately to bed.

"I don't want to talk about it," Anthony whispered. "Let's not spoil this moment. I'll just say you were right. It was all of the toads at once—and there was competition."

"So, you don't know if you got the part."

"I know I didn't get the part."

"You were told that?"

"I didn't have to be told that. I was about to be doubled and suddenly I couldn't take any more. I rolled out of the position before the second guy could spike me, stumbled down the stairs and gathered up my clothes in the living room—don't ask about that—and left."

"You left? You gave up your chance?"

"It won't be my only chance. But screw *Danny's Choice*. I bet it's never made. I bet that Atkins and his so-called investors just have a club for screwing young men. I can only have so many choices. I chose this. You. You and this. These are my choices . . . Anthony's choices."

"I think we can still make use of the book," Manuel said, reaching over to the nightstand for it.

"Kiss my nips," I heard him say, and I pulled my face into his hairy chest and kissed one of his nipples after brushing the hair aside with my tongue. "Yes, lick them. The other one too." His shirt front was wide open, his muscular, hairy chest pushing out at me. "Bite them lightly. Oh, fuck. Yes, yes." They were engorged, hard. I felt him shudder. And maybe ejaculate? No, maybe not. Would I be able to tell when he had?

I lost contact with the nipples and was arching my back and crying out to the ceiling because he was slamming me up and down on his dick with the hands gripping my waist in response to my having followed his command and fired up his arousal.

This didn't last for long, though. He slowed down and dipped his face to my chest and did the same with my nipples that he had commanded me to do to his. "Perfection," he murmured. "Young, sleek body. Dancer's body. Just the right hard muscling. Nips are hard too. You like this."

And I did like it. For the first time, I was whispering, "Yes, yes, like that," and moaning a moan of pleasure. And I felt my ass muscles relax even more. He no longer was too taxing for me down there. He moved his face up to mine and took my mouth in a deep kiss. I sighed behind the possession and, involuntarily, my channel was coming to a life of its own, caressing the shaft inside it, my pelvis beginning to move, almost imperceptibly. Rising and falling on the dick, sliding up and down on it, caressing it. So this is what those I'd asked about sex meant about how glorious it could be to be fucked.

Anthony had bent into Manuel, who was leaning his torso back on one elbow as he read, and was kissing and nipping at Manuel's nipples. He felt Manuel's shaft inside him, swollen now as never before, stretching Anthony's channel walls, and throbbing, throbbing.

"Oh, fuck, yes," Anthony murmured as Manuel's hips started in motion.

~

About the Author

Habu is one of the pen names of a former supersonic spy jet pilot, intelligence agent, male model, movie actor, and diplomat. A wild youth in South East Asia was spent enjoying whatever sexual opportunities came his way, and much of his gay male writing is about recalling incidents from those days and inventing ones he'd perhaps have liked to experience. He now leads a very quiet and ordinary happily married family life.

An American, he is a published mainstream novelist and short story writer under another name and in another dimension of his life. He has written or cowritten (with Sabb) approaching 1,000 published short stories and over 100 published erotica e-books, primarily of gay fiction but also memoir, straight fiction and ménage fiction. His hand and creative writing can be seen in stories and books by habu, sr71plt, Dirk Hessian, Shabbu, and Stephen Kessel— among unrevealed others that might surprise readers. The fictionalized GM memoir *Flying High, Diving Deep* is loosely based on his life experiences. He can be found at the adults only gay male website www.barbarianspy.com, which he shares with other BarbarianSpy authors including Sabb, Dirk Hessian, and Alex Lockheed.

Our authors always like to receive feedback, and appreciate it when readers post reviews at distributors and other sites.

BarbarianSpy

FOR LITERARY HEAT

Not all books listed below may currently be on release.
* indicates the book is available in paperback and e-book.

BOOKS BY CHRIS CROSS

Multisexual Adult Romance

Pulaski Square
Chocolate in Vanilla (MF)
Christmas with Chris (MMF) (MM) (MF)

BOOKS BY ALEX LOCKHEED

Transgender Romance

Meeting Jenna

Transgender Other

Being Sarah

BOOKS BY DIRK HESSIAN

Xtreme Historical Erotica

The King's Men
Shores of Tripoli
Prophecy of Noto
Pretender's Fate

General Historical Erotic Romance

Puttin on the Ritz
To the Hessian Hills
Fire Down the Valley*
Constantinople*
The Beautiful Way*
Blue and Gray
Colonel's Treasure
Beginning of Time
Labyrinth

BOOKS BY HABU

Gay Erotica
Memoir Faction

Flying High, Diving Deep*

Xtreme Erotica

Liaisons
Chain Gang Banged (Short Story)
Tramp Steaming*
Escape to Girne
Silas' Choice*
Last Call
Choke Hold
Apyko: The Greek Pimp
Visits of the Schlange
Second Coming: Emile La Cour Unleashed*
Vortex: Sacrificed by Curiosity*
Dark Angel Sounding *(in e-book & included in*
*Sounding:Ultimate Control paperback)**
Sounding: Ultimate Control (*Print Only*)*
Sounding Five *(in e-book & included in*
Sounding:Ultimate Control paperback)*
Romance
Finding a New Sam
Bangkok Summer Seduction
The Photograph
Inevitable Case
Turn to Love
Rain Check
Built for Pleasure (Sci Fi)*
Danny's Choice*
Pull of the Groove
Sugar n Spice Christmas
Friday Nights with Lenny (Christmas Romance)
Snowy, Snowy Nights (Christmas Romance)
Tank n Bull
Sail to the Sun
War Letters
Ravens Roost
Caribbean Cruise Top to Bottom
Arena Stage
Trading Partners (Valentine's Day)
Four Coins
Lower Than the Heart (Valentine's Day)

Brambleton
Gotta Keep Trying
Finding Amnad
Platres Conclave
Other Novels/Novellas
Syrian Ram
Temptation's Clutches*
Descent into Chaos
Escape to Girne
Journey Through Abilene
Harmony and Dissonance
Stallion Station
Racing With the Devil (espionage suspense)
Prepared in Cape Verdi
Gilded Cage
House on Park*
Anything for Ambition
Dance of the Ravishers
Hard Knocks U*
My Neighbor's Spa*
Man's Man: Tales of a High Priced Gay Hooker*
Trip Money
The Indian Doctor
Sailorboy
Home to Fire Island
Murder Mysteries
Inevitable Case
Vanishing Laura
Death on a Ping Pong Table
Clint Folsom Mysteries Compendium Volume 1*
Death to Blonds - Stolen Judgment (Clint Folsom
Mystery)*
Clint Folsom Mysteries Compendium Volume 2*
Gay Erotica Anthologies
Earth Cry*
Shunga
Habu's Christmas Balls
Eight in D*

DevilMENt
Silas' Choices*
Stallion Station (A Novella in Parts)
Eleven to the Dogs*
Fifty Seventy*
Spy Tails 001*
Spy Tails 002*
Doubled*
Doubled Again*
Tails in the Tropics*
Tails in the Med*
Tails in the West*
Rough Riders*
Grab Bag 1*
Grab Bag 2*
Grab Bag 3*
Grab Bag 4*
Grab Bag 5*
Grab Bag 6*
Grab Bag 7*
Grab Bag 8*
Grab Bag 9*
Beyond the Beaded Curtain*
Habu's Christmas Balls
The Sporting Life*
Fetish Galore!*
Literary Gay Erotica
Cairo Surrender*
The Handyman*
Homeward Bound
Journey to Mirage*
Bisexual/Menage/Multisexual Erotica
And Eat it Too
Two Men, One Woman*
Every Which Way
Summer of Denial
Death on a Ping Pong Table
Cruising Gigolo

13 Ways for Halloween
Luther*
The Indian Prince*
BOOKS BY SABB
Driver Reliever
Hiring in Hollywood
The Legend of Holleystone Grange
Surprise Encounters*
She is He
Wrong Man
Loyal to his King
Barbarian Tales - Book One - Traveler's Tales*
Barbarian Tales - Book Two - Journeys Begin*
Barbarian Tales - Book Three - The Inheritance*
Barbarian Tales - Book Four - Road to Persepolis*
BOOKS BY SHABBU
Velvet Interrogation
Finding Jason
Dirty Pool
Operation Black Jade
Cigars!*
Angel in the Barn
Gayly Complicated*
Despoiling David
The Tree of Idleness*
I Met a Man
Rough Road to Happiness
BOOKS BY STEPHEN KESSEL
Gay Romance
The Forever Man
Two Chances
BOOKS BY KIM BLACK
Lesbian Romance
Transfixed on Tammie (F/T lesbian)

www.ingramcontent.com/pod-product-compliance
Lightning Source LLC
Chambersburg PA
CBHW022037170626
46808CB00003B/1236